I won't forg

That night, Cathy (

This time, in her dream, she stood once more in the graveyard where Jennie was buried. Grass had sprouted from the grave, under the tombstone that read JENNIFER MARIE BRODIE, BELOVED DAUGHTER. THE MAIDEN IS NOT DEAD, BUT SLEEPETH.

Abruptly, the landscape wavered and changed— from the springtime cemetery to the bare trees and brown, withered grass of Johnson's Swamp. Ragged clouds scudded by overhead on a cold autumn wind, just as they had on that day when the hunters had found Jennie's body.

Then, from beyond the trees, Cathy heard a girl's voice, screaming and sobbing. Between the cries and sobs came the same words repeated over and over: *"Oh, no, help me! Help me!"*

It was Jennie's voice. Cathy stood, frozen, while the screaming died away. After a long-drawn-out, silent pause, the bushes under the trees began to shake and rustle, as if some big clumsy animal were trying to move through them.

Then the thing emerged, and Cathy began to scream herself.

BOOKS IN THE HORROR HIGH SERIES
AVAILABLE FROM BOXTREE

1. Hard Rock
2. Sudden Death
3. Blood Game

And coming soon:

4. Final Curtain
5. Deadly Secret
6. Voice of Evil
7. You're Dead
8. Heartbreaker

HORROR HIGH

BLOOD GAME

Nicholas Adams

B☉XTREE

First published in the UK 1993
by BOXTREE LIMITED, Broadwall House,
21 Broadwall, London SE1 9PL

First published in the USA 1991 by HarperPaperbacks,
A Division of HarperCollins*Publishers*,
10 East 53rd Street, New York, N.Y. 10022

10 9 8 7 6 5 4 3 2 1

Cover art by Paul Campion
Cover design by Head

1–85283–832–9

Printed and bound in Great Britain by
Cox & Wyman, Reading, Berkshire

A catalogue record for this book is available from the British Library

Chapter 1

Cathy Atmore hurried up the steps of Cresswell High. Even though the sky was a bright October blue, the chilly wind whipping through her short brown curls made her wish she'd worn a hat. But wearing a hat in the morning would have given her flat, bounceless "hat hair" for the rest of the day. She didn't need that. It was bad enough that she had a plain face behind glasses thicker than the bottom of a Coca-Cola bottle.

Inside, she joined the other students already surging through the halls of the old brick school building. Cresswell High had a student body of well over a thousand—few enough that the students knew each other by sight, but too many for anyone but Mr. Cooder, the school secretary, to know all their names.

Inside the school, locker doors banged and crashed as the students hung up their coats. Cathy walked through the crowded hallways, hurrying to get to her locker and then to homeroom. She waved to her friend Cheryl Barkham, but she didn't dare stop to chat so close to the final bell.

1

Cheryl was more like an acquaintance anyway, not a close friend like Jennifer Brodie. Jennie had been Cathy's best friend all through grade school, as well as her next-door neighbor, until Mr. Brodie struck it rich with his string of Lucky Chicken franchises. Then the Brodies had moved out of the Upper Basin district and into a beautiful colonial-style house in Gaspee Farms.

Cathy would have stopped to talk with Jennie even if it did make her miss the bell. Jennie hadn't abandoned *her*—the short kid in glasses from the unfashionable part of town—even after Jennie had developed into the popular, good-looking star of the senior cheerleading squad.

Cathy needed to talk with Jennie today. She hadn't seen her since the party Friday night—a noisy, crowded after-the-game celebration at Eric Skidwell's house in Rocky Banks Estates—the sort of thing Cathy got invited to every once in a while because she was Jennie's friend. Jennie had wanted to talk about something that night; she'd told Cathy so, but then her boyfriend, Don Fulman, had come up and hauled Jennie off to dance in the room with the stereo. Cathy had hoped they would have a chance to talk later, but she'd had to leave the party early, before Jennie came back.

Cathy made it into her homeroom just as the last bell rang. Mrs. Pangborn started calling the roll and marking the absences on the slip for the school office.

Cathy answered "Here" when her name was

called, without looking up from her history notebook. Mr. Osgood's American history class was first period, and she had to prepare for it now. Osgood never smiled before about two in the afternoon, but history would have been Cathy's least favorite subject even at a better time of day. She usually looked over her notes and reread the assigned material during homeroom.

She bit her lip, noticing for the first time since Friday that there had been an assignment over the weekend—one that she hadn't bothered to do, hadn't even remembered until this moment: a one-page report on the Dred Scott decision. *Too bad I don't have a dog,* Cathy thought. *Then I could say the dog ate it.*

Then she shrugged. The assignment didn't matter except to her own sense of self-respect; her grades were good enough that she could slide by with a B or even a C in American history and not worry. As long as she got her diploma, the transcripts for her first three years—plus her SAT scores—were all that any college would ever see.

She'd done pretty well on the SAT, too. In fact, Cathy was one of the brains of Cresswell High, at least according to her friend Jennie. Not that being a brain had kept Cathy from forgetting all about that stupid history paper. Now she'd have to listen to Osgood the Grouch as a morning warm-up. Mr. Osgood had a way of talking, quiet and sarcastic, that could make people feel like dirt if they did something he disliked. And not doing homework was up near the top of the list of things he didn't like.

Cheryl Barkham leaned over from the next desk. "Have you seen Henry O'Toole this morning? He's wearing a black shirt and a white tie and a fedora! He looks like a TV gangster."

Cathy shook her head. "What some people won't do to get noticed."

Henry was always doing something, she reflected —usually something weird, and sometimes something obnoxious. But he was mostly harmless, unlike that creep Mel Downing, who would stand too close and stare down her blouse, even if it was buttoned up to her neck. The things girls had to put up with . . .

She returned to her history book. No, a report hadn't magically appeared tucked inside the back cover. Maybe Mr. Osgood wouldn't be here today, and they'd have a substitute. Maybe the roof would fall in. Maybe—there went the bell. Time to go to class.

The roof hadn't fallen in on the history room, and they didn't have a substitute, either. Everything was just as it always was: the world map on one wall, the dusty flags of a dozen countries tacked around near the ceiling, the rows of flimsy-looking desks. And Mr. Osgood in his three-piece suit standing with his hands in his pockets up at the front. The bell rang again just as Cathy sat down.

"Good morning, class," Mr. Osgood began. "I hope you had a pleasant and productive weekend."

4

He didn't look as if he hoped any such thing. "Please pass your homework papers forward."

Cathy rustled in her notebook, trying to look as if she had something to turn in. No use letting Osgood get started on her any sooner than he had to. She was so intent on finding the nonexistent paper that she missed the first words of the announcement that crackled over the intercom.

". . . following students report to the office at once," said the dry voice of Mr. Cooder. "George Jacobs. Franklin Reed. Eric Skidwell. Donald Fulman. Todd Barber. Sylvia Roper. Cheryl Barkham. Pamela Greeley. Matthew Wilcox. Linda Sturgess. Susan De Sica. Cathy Atmore . . ."

Cathy Atmore! That was her!

"Have to go to the office," she said. She scooped up her books and hurried out before Mr. Osgood could stop her. She was so relieved that she wouldn't get caught without her assignment that she didn't wonder why she'd been called to the office until she was down in Cresswell High's big, echoing lobby.

The lobby seemed even larger than usual without a throng of people coming and going. A row of chairs had been set up along one wall of the corridor, and several students were already waiting there. Cheryl sat in one of the chairs, and Don Fulman was sitting in another.

Cathy recognized most of the other students. They were all friends of hers—well, she admitted, not close friends exactly. Just people she knew and whose parties she sometimes went to because of knowing Jennie. Most of Jennie's crowd these days lived in Gaspee Farms and Rocky Banks Estates and had parents who were doctors and lawyers. Cathy lived in the Upper Basin and had a father who drove eighteen-wheelers up and down the coast for a living.

"What's going on?" Cathy whispered as she walked past Cheryl's seat.

Cheryl shrugged. "Don't know."

Cathy went into the office. "I'm here, Mr. Cooder."

The school secretary was the sort of man you'd expect to wear a bow tie, but he didn't. His hair was gray and he never smiled or joked with the students. Today, he was holding a clipboard. He made a mark on the clipboard, then looked at her.

"Cathy Atmore," he said. "Take a seat in the hall with the others."

"What's this all about?" Cathy asked.

"Take a seat," Mr. Cooder repeated. "Wait until you're called."

She went back outside and sat down next to Cheryl. Taking a sheet of paper out of her notebook, she went to work paraphrasing what her history textbook said about Dred Scott.

Time passed. Don Fulman sprawled in a chair on the other side of the corridor. After a while he stuck his feet out in front of him and yawned, covering his mouth with the back of his hand. Cathy went on writing.

Suddenly, she was aware of Mr. Cooder standing

in front of her. "Miss Atmore," he said, "please pay attention. This is the second time I have been forced to call your name."

He indicated one of the inner doors inside the main office. The brass nameplate on the door said HENRY LIPTON, ASSISTANT PRINCIPAL. "Through there," he said.

Cathy walked in, clutching her books. Something funny was going on. Mr. Lipton was in charge of student discipline at Cresswell, and he had bigger stuff to worry about than anything she might have done lately.

The next surprise was waiting inside. Mr. Lipton sat in a chair to one side, busying himself with some papers in his lap. A strange man sat behind the desk. He had a bulging manila folder, a thick legal pad, and a portable tape recorder.

The man looked up. He was thin, with brown hair and a deeply creased face. In the light from the windows behind him, a thin swatch of stubble showed along one side of his jaw, as if he had shaved in a hurry this morning. He tapped the recorder, and it began to whir.

"Take a seat, Miss"—he looked down at his note pad—"Atmore."

Cathy sat.

"My name is Detective Rogers, Cresswell Police Department. I have a few questions for you."

"Yes, sir," Cathy said.

"First I'd like you to look at this photo," said the detective. "Do you recognize this person?"

He pulled a picture out of his folder and pushed it across the desk. Cathy leaned forward and picked it up. The picture was from last year's Cresswell High yearbook. It showed a blond girl in a cheerleader's letter sweater smiling at the camera.

"Yes," Cathy said. "That's Jennie. Jennifer Brodie."

"How well do you know Miss Brodie?"

"She's my best friend," Cathy said. Her uneasiness grew stronger. "Is something wrong?" she asked. "Is Jennie okay?"

"Just answer the questions, please," Detective Rogers replied. "How long have you known Miss Brodie?"

"Since first grade, at least," Cathy said. "Please, sir, what's the—"

"When was the last time you saw Miss Brodie?" Rogers cut in, his face expressionless.

"Last Friday," Cathy answered. "Friday night."

"About what time?"

"Nine or nine-thirty," she said. "I don't remember exactly. We were at a party."

"Where would that have been?"

"At Eric's house."

The detective looked at his notebook. "Eric Skidwell?"

Cathy nodded. "He's on the football team, and the party was to celebrate winning the game against Arnold High. We lost, but he went on with the party anyway."

"I see," the detective said. "And who else was there?"

The questioning seemed to go on and on. Had Jennie come to the party alone? Did she leave alone? Did she seem happy? Sad? Worried? Who were her friends? Who were her enemies?

Cathy answered the questions the best she could, and all the time the sinking feeling in the pit of her stomach grew stronger—worse than not doing her homework, worse than not knowing the answers on a test.

She didn't know what to say about enemies. Jennie didn't have enemies—everyone in the school wanted to be her friend. She used to laugh about it. And Jennie liked being everyone's friend, too.

"Do you think that Miss Brodie might talk to strangers?" Yes, she might; she'd talk to anybody, even nerds like Stu Martin and Bill Madsen, who spent most of their time communing with the keyboards down in the computer lab. "Did you see any strangers around the party?" No, not that Cathy recalled. "Did Miss Brodie mention meeting any strangers over the last couple of weeks?" No, Jennie hadn't. "Did Miss Brodie try to get in touch with you at any time over the weekend?" Not that Cathy knew of; she'd been in Fall River with her mother from Saturday morning until Sunday night.

At last the detective looked up from his notebook. "Thank you very much for your cooperation, Miss—ah, Atmore. If you think of anything else to tell me, you can reach me at this number." He handed across a business card with his name and the detective bureau number printed on it. Cathy slipped the card into her purse.

"That will be all," said the detective. "Please ask Mr. Cooder to send in the next student."

Numbly, Cathy stood up and turned to go.

She walked out into the hall where Mr. Cooder was waiting. As soon as Cathy came through the door, Mr. Cooder pointed with his pencil at Linda Sturgess.

"Next," he said. Linda went into the assistant principal's office.

Cathy made her way to the second floor and Mr. Osgood's room. She was halfway to her seat before she noticed that she was in the wrong class, and she retreated, embarrassed, amid the sound of laughter.

The bell for the end of first period must have rung while she was with the detective, and she hadn't even noticed. She went on to her second-period math class, and even though she'd done all the homework here—she enjoyed math, and she was good at it—she didn't hear a word the teacher said all period. She couldn't wrench her thoughts away from the image of the police detective, asking his patient questions down in the assistant principal's office.

And those questions, all about friends and enemies and when-did-you-see-her-last—Detective Rogers wouldn't be asking questions like that if everything were okay. Something was wrong. Something had happened to Jennie Brodie.

Chapter 2

Lunchtime came, and Cathy still didn't know what was going on. She hadn't seen Jennie anywhere, not in any classes or in the halls. On her way to the cafeteria, she tried calling the Brodies' house from one of the school's pay telephones, but nobody was home—all she got was the answering machine, with Jennie's cheerful recorded voice saying, *"Hi! You've reached the Brodie residence. We're not home right now, but you can leave your message at the sound of the beep, and we'll get right back to you!"*

Cathy hung up without saying anything. She went on down to the school cafeteria, even though she didn't have much appetite, and got a salad and a fruit plate from the cold-lunch counter.

The cafeteria was a noisy, crowded room where the smell of French fries and chili from the fast-food line mingled with the odor of overcooked steam-table cabbage off the regular menu. Cathy took her red plastic tray and went over to the section where she usually sat.

She slid into her habitual place, but this time Jennie wasn't there to take the chair across from her, and nobody spoke up to greet her. Instead, the kids sitting at her table were oddly silent. Looking around, Cathy saw that they were the same ones who'd been sitting in the hallway that morning.

Todd Barber showed up a few moments later. "Well," he said as he sat down, "here we all are— Mister Rogers's Neighborhood."

A couple of people laughed kind of halfheartedly. But it was true, Cathy thought. Except for her—and Jennie—most of these people lived within a mile or so of each other, in the same part of Rocky Banks Estates.

"What do you think he wanted?" Pam Greeley asked.

Pam was another member of the cheerleading squad, a voluptuous brunette. Her boyfriend was Eric Skidwell, the host of Friday night's party. Eric wasn't at the table yet, so Pam was actually talking with other people.

"Beats me," said Joey Dillman, of the track team. "The cop was asking about Jennie. I told him I hadn't seen her since Friday."

"Same thing I told him," Linda Sturgess said.

"We all told him that," Todd said. "I know I haven't seen her since Eric's party."

"Do you suppose something happened to her?"

That was Stacy, Pam's best friend. If Jennie was the best-liked member of the cheerleading squad, then Stacy was the group's fashion-setter. Whatever Stacy did, Pam followed suit, and the rest of the cheerleaders did the same the week after.

Take the red-and-blue scarf Stacy was wearing this morning. She'd been the first to get one, and now Pam and half the other girls had scarves just like it. Even Jennie had finally gotten a scarf like that. It was like a badge, Cathy decided, something to show the world that you were part of the "in" crowd at Cresswell High.

Before anyone could answer Stacy's question, however, Don Fulman joined the group. Jennie's boyfriend collapsed his powerful body into a chair and crashed his tray onto the table the way he always did. He looked tired, and Cathy wondered how long the detective had spent questioning him.

She wasn't the only one who was curious—the others at the table were all watching Don, too. Todd Barber was the first to speak.

"How'd things go between you and our pal Detective Rogers?"

"I didn't tell him anything," Don said. He took a bite of his burger, chewed it carefully, swallowed, then drank a swig of milk before he continued. "If they want to ask me a bunch of questions, fine, but they don't get answers. Not unless they arrest me first. So I ask him, 'Are you accusing me of something?' and he says, 'No.' 'Great,' I tell him. 'Then I've got nothing to say to you.' "

Don reached into his shirt pocket and pulled out a little rectangle of white cardboard. Cathy recognized it as the business card that Detective Rogers must have given to Don.

"Here's what I think about that detective," said

Don. While the others watched, he tore the card in half, then into quarters, and he went on ripping until he had nothing left but a handful of shredded cardboard. He dropped the fragments onto his tray, then looked around the table, his dark features suddenly intense.

"The rest of you," he said, "ought to do the same thing. The cops aren't our friends."

There was a moment of silence. Then Todd pulled the detective's business card out of his notebook. A few seconds later, Pam and Stacy had their cards out as well. All at once, the other kids were destroying their little rectangles of cardboard. The torn pieces drifted down onto the table like falling leaves.

Cathy looked down at her uneaten fruit plate. "I lost mine," she mumbled to nobody in particular.

It was a lie—the card was still tucked inside her purse—but she couldn't think of anything else to say. No matter how much she didn't want to stand out in the crowd, she couldn't bring herself to destroy her link to someone who might be trying to help Jennie.

Don's next words made her feel as if he'd been reading her mind. "You guys who spilled your guts to that cop," he said, looking straight at Cathy, "you've got to remember, he isn't in there for Jennie, and he isn't in there for you. He's in there for himself."

"Those questions he was asking," Cathy finally gathered enough nerve to say, "they sure sounded like he was trying to help Jennie."

14

"Or to arrest her," Don said. "Did you think about that? You talk to a cop, you'd better have a lawyer with you."

Cathy fell silent. She'd never been very good at arguing face-to-face with forceful types like Don Fulman. She didn't say anything more, and she sat picking at her salad while everybody else traded guesses back and forth about what the police had really wanted.

She wasn't interested in the conversation, anyhow. None of these people were pleasant to be with when Jennie wasn't around—Jennie had a way of making whoever she was with seem nicer than they really were.

Even me, Cathy admitted. *Without Jennie, I'd be spending all my time in the computer lab with the rest of the nerds.*

The rest of the day passed in a blur of worry and gossip. It seemed as if the whole school knew that the cops had been talking to the people in Jennifer Brodie's crowd, and everybody had a different theory about what was going on. By the time Cathy rode home on the cross-town bus, she felt tired, headachy, and sickened by the half-eager, half-frightened questions that seemed to follow her wherever she went, because she'd been one of the ones who'd gotten interviewed.

On the bus she found a seat away from the other high school students. She leaned against the cool glass of the bus window and closed her eyes. If this had been a normal day, she might have gotten a ride home with Jennie—it seemed as if lately most of the football players and cheerleaders had been getting their own cars, and Jennie was no exception.

Cathy still had a headache when she got off at the bus stop in the Upper Basin. The district where she and Jennie had grown up had once been a high-class neighborhood where tall shade trees lined the streets between between two- and three-story Victorian houses. These days, however, a faint but unmistakable air of decay hung over everything. The knobby roots of the great trees had pushed up through the sidewalk years ago, and too many of the elegant old homes had cracked windows and peeling paint.

The Atmores rented a gray three-story house that had been split in half down the middle to make room for two families. Cathy lived with her mother and father in the right-hand side. Cathy opened the storm door, unlocked the main door, and walked in.

"Cathy?" called her mother from upstairs. "Is that you?"

"Yes, Mom," Cathy called back. She and her mother were alone in the house right now—her father was on the road, and he wouldn't be back for another two days. "I'm home."

Mrs. Atmore came out onto the upstairs landing, her arms full of folded laundry. "How was school?"

"A policeman was there," said Cathy, "asking questions about Jennie."

Cathy's mother frowned. "Oh, dear. Is she in trouble?"

"I don't know what's wrong," said Cathy. "She

wasn't in school. The detective kept wanting to know what she'd been doing this weekend. Was I with her, had I seen her with anyone—stuff like that."

"Oh," said Mrs. Atmore. She looked troubled. "Did you tell him we were in Fall River the whole time?"

"Yes, Mom," said Cathy.

Mrs. Atmore's expression cleared. "That's all right, then. I hope everything's okay," she said, and went back into the bedroom. Cathy wandered into the living room and switched on the TV.

Her headache had faded, leaving her feeling restless and uneasy. She sat down on the big, comfortable couch with its homemade floral slipcovers and tried to watch one of the late-afternoon soap operas. When she realized she couldn't follow the characters' conversations, she gave up and started doing her homework. But she couldn't concentrate on that, either.

She was almost relieved when the local news came on at five o'clock. After the opening music and the commercials, the first story began with the station's roving reporter standing in front of a clump of trees. Police cars sat in the background, their blue rooflights blinking.

"Two hunters made a grisly discovery this morning in Johnson's Swamp," the reporter was saying. "The body of a teenage girl."

The picture changed to a pair of men clutching shotguns, standing beneath a gray, dawn-lit sky. A

17

banner across the bottom of the screen read TAPED EARLIER TODAY.

"Yep," one of the men was saying, "Bert and I was just going down to the swamp looking to shoot a duck or so, and when we got into the bushes, there she was."

Oh, no, Cathy thought. *Not Jennie . . . please let it not be Jennie!*

The picture changed again, this time to what looked like early afternoon, although the TAPED EARLIER banner continued to run. Now four sheriff's deputies were carrying a black plastic body bag out of the woods. A man in a rumpled suit stood by the reporter—Detective Rogers.

"We have a good idea of what happened here," Rogers said. His voice sounded just as it had that morning, flat and unexpressive. "Our inquiry will be straightforward."

Again the picture changed, and the banner underneath shifted to read LIVE. Once more the reporter stood alone. "Police investigation continues at this hour," he said, "into the murder of Jennifer Brodie. Brodie, a senior at Cresswell High School, was a popular member of the cheerleading squad. . . ."

Cathy stood and walked to the TV. She switched the picture off and squeezed her eyes shut. It didn't help. She could still see those four deputies carrying the body bag out of the trees.

She stumbled to the couch and sat down. How could this have happened to someone like Jennie?

The phone was on the end table by the couch. Cathy picked up the receiver and dialed the Brodies' number, just to hear Jennie's voice again.

"Hi! You've reached the Brodie residence. . . ."

She waited until after the beep. Then she said, "I love you, Jennie," and hung up.

She sat on the couch for a long time, not doing anything, just sitting. Finally the phone rang. It was Cheryl.

"Cath—did you hear about Jennie?" Cheryl asked.

"Yes," Cathy replied. *She must have heard the news at work.* Cheryl had an after-school job over at the Hair Today beauty parlor.

"It's all they're talking about at the salon," Cheryl said. "That cop at school today—"

"Didn't say what was wrong," Cathy said. *But he knew about this the whole time. He knew Jennie was lying there dead, and he didn't tell me.* She wished Cheryl would hang up and leave her alone. "All I know is what I heard on the news."

Cheryl wasn't about to let the subject go, however. "Did the news report tell *everything* about her?"

"No . . . I don't know," Cathy said numbly. Suddenly, her glasses weren't working too well. She took them off, and the room turned into a comforting blur.

"A lady who was in today was one of those hunters' wives or something," Cheryl went on, sounding excited and horrified. "And *she* said that Jennie was all cut up, with pieces of her everywhere! I'm really sorry, Cath. I know she was your best friend."

Cathy didn't say anything. She put the handset onto her chest and looked vacantly at the fuzzy shapes of the living room. The vibrations in the plastic under her hand told her that Cheryl was still talking. Cathy hung up, cutting Cheryl off, and sat on the couch while the room grew dim around her.

At last she put her glasses on again, walked over to the TV, and flipped it back on. The national news was showing. Cathy watched it to the end, until a little one-minute spot from the local channel came on. "Police have announced that they have a prime suspect in the mutilation/murder of Jennifer Brodie. Details at eleven."

She turned the TV off. Her mother's voice broke into the silence. "Cathy, dear, dinnertime."

Cathy made it in to dinner, but she couldn't eat.

After a minute, Mrs. Atmore pushed back her hair and leaned over to put her hand on Cathy's. "I'm so sorry, honey. I heard the news upstairs. I don't know what to say. We've known Jennie since she was a little girl. And now she's gone." Cathy's mother paused, but Cathy just looked down at her cold and congealing dinner. "You don't have to eat, sweetheart. Would you rather go lie down? Maybe you'd like some hot tea later."

Cathy nodded dumbly, then stood up. Her mother stood, too, and hugged her briefly, hard.

Then Cathy went upstairs to her room and

flopped face forward on her bed in the dark. She didn't undress. After a while, she slept.

She woke suddenly. She had heard a voice.

Then sanity took over, and she knew she had been dreaming. But for a moment, it had felt so real —a voice, Jennie's voice, whispering frightened and low.

"Cath, you've got to help me! I need you."

Chapter 3

Bill Madsen, Jr., drove his beat-up Ford into the parking lot of Cranmer Memorial Hospital, where his mother worked. His pale gray eyes narrowed thoughtfully behind his horn-rimmed glasses as he considered the news report he'd heard on the way over.

So the missing Jennifer Brodie was now officially the late Jennifer Brodie. He wasn't surprised. He'd been expecting an announcement like that for a while now. He'd been mildly amused, this morning, to see most of the smart set at Cresswell High sitting outside the principal's office waiting to talk to the police detective. Bill's name hadn't been on the detective's list. He wasn't part of that crowd—the athletes and cheerleaders and their hangers-on—and if Jennie Brodie had sometimes talked to him, it was because Jennie would talk to anyone.

Just the same, Bill reflected, the police ought to have called him in for questioning. After all, the party Friday night had been next door to his own house, even if he hadn't been invited. He didn't get invitations to the parties that Jennie went to—in fact, he seldom got invited to parties at all. But there were things he could have told them. He'd heard voices and music coming from the Skidwells' house all that evening, so loud that if Dr. William Madsen, Sr., hadn't been out of town at a medical convention, he would have called the cops to lodge a complaint.

Although the Madsens lived in the exclusive Rocky Banks Estates, Bill himself had never fit in with the well-off, well-groomed clique of Rocky Banks students at Cresswell High. By the time his family had moved into town from Baltimore two years ago, the kids at Cresswell had already settled down in friendships that would last through high school, and outsiders weren't particularly welcome.

Somebody with lots of self-confidence or with talent for a flashy, attention-getting activity like football might have broken into the closed ranks. Bill didn't make it in either category, and he didn't see any point in trying. His only after-school activity was his membership in the Hackers' Club—a handful of computer enthusiasts, without officers, by-laws, or organized activities, who gathered at irregular intervals in the basement room where the machines were set up.

Bill's parents were both doctors, his father a dermatologist in private practice, and his mother a pathologist at Cranmer Memorial. When Dr. Elizabeth Madsen's Saab refused to start on Friday afternoon, she'd promptly made an appointment to have it towed to the shop the next morning for repairs and a tuneup. Bill had driven her down to the hospital that same evening for her overnight shift, and with his father—and his father's car—still out of town, he'd been dropping his mother off and picking her up for three days now. He parked his Ford in the parking lot by the new wing, then headed for the basement, where Dr. Madsen had her office.

He went straight past the bio-chem lab, past the hematology lab with its centrifuge and racks of red-filled test tubes, and down to the pathologists' branch at the end, where the hospital smells of soap and disinfectant were always the strongest. There, beyond the steel doors of the morgue, Dr. Elizabeth Madsen examined the work of other doctors—sometimes after they'd succeeded, as when she tested an appendix to make sure it had in fact been diseased when it was removed, but more often after the doctors had failed. Then she would perform the autopsy that determined the true cause of death.

Bill took a shortcut through the pathologists' storeroom, where glass jars held body parts preserved in clear liquid. Bill lingered there occasionally, drawn by a morbid fascination with the discarded bits and pieces of humanity in their sealed containers—a human hand floating in its jar like a bleached crab, a liver mottled with cirrhosis, an eyeball with a warty tumor protruding from its back. Tonight, though, he went through the storeroom without pausing and into his mother's office.

No one was there. He settled down behind her desk to wait for her. Tonight he was early. He waited a bit longer, then started looking for something to read.

A copy of the *Journal of Blood Diseases* lay on top of the desk. He picked it up and flipped through it, glancing at the captions on the advertisements. Most of the *Journal* was ads. He put the magazine down and looked for something more interesting. Boredom had been Bill's major problem ever since moving to Cresswell—very little that came his way provided much of an intellectual challenge for very long.

Here was something. A manila folder with a name on the tab. BRODIE, JENNIFER MARIE. He hesitated a minute, listening for voices or footsteps in the corridor outside, then pulled the folder over to him, opened it, and began to read.

It was an autopsy report. The dry prose and medical terms didn't slow him down—he'd heard his parents talk shop all his life. He knew what *exsanguination* meant, listed down on the "Conclusions" line: Jennie had bled to death after the veins and arteries in her neck had been severed with a sharp, single-edged implement. And that was only the first of the nasty things that had happened to Jennie Brodie.

Bill nodded to himself. The autopsy was very thorough, but then, his mom did excellent work. She wouldn't have missed a thing.

He shut the folder and replaced it exactly where he'd found it. Mom would be pretty upset if she caught him looking through her private papers. He leaned back and closed his eyes.

Dr. Madsen arrived a couple of minutes later. She took off her white coat and hung it on the hook behind the door.

"Hi, honey," she said. "Ready to go?"

"Ready and willing, Mom," he replied.

The folder stayed behind on the desk. The next morning at school, waiting for the first bell in the company of fellow computer nuts Stu Martin and Larry Davidson, Bill couldn't resist the temptation to pass along some of the details he knew. Details that hadn't been mentioned on the evening news.

Bill swore Stu and Larry to secrecy, of course, but the story was all over Cresswell High in a flash—whispered from friend to friend in the halls, scrawled on slips of paper passed from hand to hand in class. By midmorning, everybody knew: Jennifer Brodie's legs were missing, and the police still hadn't found them.

The mood at Cresswell on Tuesday was nervous and unhappy. Students huddled together in little groups, talking in hushed voices and looking uneasily at each other. Cathy saw one girl weeping—a transfer student from Arnold High whom Jennie had barely known.

Not everybody seemed upset, however. At lunch in the cafeteria, Henry O'Toole looked down at his helping of Breaded Veal Cutlet. He tasted a bite.

"Well," he said, "now we know what happened to

Brodie's legs!" Then he leaned back in his chair and started to sing softly, to the tune of "The Battle Hymn of the Republic":

"Jennie Brodie's bloody body's bundled in a body bag,
Jennie Brodie's bloody body's bundled in a body bag,
Jennie Brodie's bloody body's bundled in a body bag,
But her legs go marching on.
Gory, gory Jennie Brodie,
Gory, gory Jennie Brodie . . ."

Henry had just started to drum on the table in rhythm when a pair of large, strong hands clamped down on his shoulders. He looked around. Don Fulman stood behind him, along with Matt and Eric and a bunch of the other football players. Don had dark circles under his eyes.

"I don't think that's very funny," Don said slowly. "My friends don't think that's very funny, either. Maybe you'd better think hard before you do anything else that isn't funny."

About then Mr. Osgood showed up. "Okay, kids, break it up," he said. He turned to Don. "I'd be careful, young man, if I were you."

"Right, right," Don muttered. He let go of Henry's shoulders and walked back toward his own table.

Over in that section of the cafeteria, Cathy

Atmore watched and listened. Cathy had spent the day wrapped in a foggy gray cocoon of unbelief. It seemed to her that the world had ended, that part of herself was no more—but all the students around her, the star athletes and the cheerleaders who should have been Jennie's closest friends, seemed to be going on as if nothing had happened.

Down at the other end of the table, two girls in blue and red scarves leaned their heads together and giggled over some private joke. Cathy was already feeling cut out of the group. She wasn't a cheerleader or an athlete—her role in the crowd had always been "Jennie's Friend." Now that Jennie was gone, the other girls were becoming less polite to Cathy, leaving her out of conversations and ignoring her in the halls. As for the guys, they never had scrambled for dates with her, except sometimes as a road to getting a date with Jennie. She supposed that was over, too—she couldn't imagine someone like Todd or Eric asking her out for any other reason.

Don came back and sat down in his chair. *He really looks rocky this morning,* Cathy thought. In spite of all his tough talk at lunch yesterday, he'd been down at the police station last night answering questions—a lot of them.

Now he gave a stormy look to everyone gathered at the table. "It's not funny," he said again.

Cathy kept watching Don, but in her mind she was seeing the party last Friday. Jennie had been wearing her new blue and red scarf knotted at the collar of her cheerleader's uniform. She'd seemed preoccupied with something, sort of worried and brooding. She'd said, "Cath, I need to talk to you," but then Don had come up, and she had changed the subject. She'd walked away laughing on her boyfriend's arm, as if nothing were wrong. And that was the last time Cathy had seen Jennie alive.

Cathy thought back even further, to the day last summer when she and Don and Jennie had been joking around in the parking lot at the Lucky Chicken. They'd talked about their senior year coming up, and their plans for getting out of this town, for going to exciting places and doing great things.

"When the time comes," Jennie had said, laughing, "I'm leaving."

Cathy remembered that Don hadn't even smiled. "If you ever try to leave *me*," he'd said flatly, "I'll kill you."

And then there was the time Don had beat up Len Pelsher just for asking Jennie for a date—never mind that Len was a creep.

Should she call Detective Rogers and tell him about what Jennie had said, or about how jealous and possessive Don could be? Cathy decided against it. Everyone knew that Don had spent the night being questioned—as a witness. As long as the police didn't accuse him of a crime, she realized, they could do almost anything. Suspects have rights; witnesses don't.

In fifth period, a study hall Cathy shared with Don, someone came to the door with a note for the supervising teacher. The teacher handed the note to

Don. Don left. A whisper ran around the room: *The cops want him again.*

After school, Cathy went down to the school's computer lab. She needed to unwind and see some friendly, or at least undemanding, faces. Lots of the computer geeks and nerds were what the school guidance counselors called "poorly socialized," which meant they spent a lot of time talking to machines because they didn't have a clue about how to talk with people. Right now, that suited Cathy just fine.

There were only three other people in the computer lab when she got there: Bill Madsen, working at his terminal transcribing class notes from a pocket tape recorder; Larry Davidson, folding paper airplanes; and Stu Martin, dodging the airplanes Larry threw. None of them looked around as Cathy came in.

Cathy was the only female member of the Hackers' Club. This had given her hopes of getting a date until she got a good look at the available talent. Bill was creepy, Stu was geeky, and Larry was two years younger than everyone else in his class and painfully shy to boot. Not counting her, the entire club had probably had about one date between them. For most of them, the dating scene was something that had a priority of zero on a scale of one to ten.

Cathy was the only person at Cresswell who'd really made the crossover between the hackers and the cheerleader crowd. A lot of the time, she felt more comfortable with the hackers—even when, as now, they were acting as if they hadn't passed kindergarten.

Stu ducked another paper airplane. He was a picture of nerdiness, a nerd's nerd, from the heavy black glasses and pocket pencil holder to the calculator and the high-water pants over white socks. "Hey, Cathy," he said, "you hear about what happened to Brodie?"

"Yeah, I heard," Cathy said. She turned her back to him and booted up one of the terminals. Trust Stu to say something he couldn't imagine would hurt her feelings. He had no idea what the word *feelings* meant. That was all right; today she was planning to do something fiddly and detailed, something that would allow her to forget the world. That was what the rest of these guys did, wasn't it? The world had rejected them, so they rejected the world right back.

"Anyway," Stu said, "we have a quorum of the club right here, right now. I say we take a vote."

"On what?" Larry asked. He folded up another sheet of green and white printout paper into an airplane.

"I say it isn't right that we don't have any athletes in the club," Stu said. "They might feel discriminated against, and that just isn't right."

"They don't want to join," Bill said, not looking up from his screen.

"No, I think they do," Stu said. "And I say we make Don Fulman an honorary member—in recognition of his brilliant hack."

Larry Davidson gave a nervous laugh. Cathy felt the blood drain from her face, leaving her pale and clammy. She stood up, shoving her chair backward so hard it fell to the floor with a crash, and even Bill Madsen looked up at the noise.

Cathy let the chair lie where it had fallen. "Stuart Martin, you are a worm," she said. She punched the *off* button on her machine and stalked out.

Chapter 4

That night, Cathy tossed and turned restlessly for a long time before she fell asleep. And when she slept, she dreamed. It was night in her dream, and she wandered around the Lower Basin.

The streets of the Lower Basin were twisty and narrow, full of dark alleys and unexpected dead-ends where empty buildings loomed on either side like fortresses made of grimy brick. The gutters ran with dirt and oil with every hard rainfall, and garbage blew up in piles against the graffiti-covered walls on windy days. Even in daylight, walking through the Lower Basin was an invitation to robbery, or worse.

In her dream, Cathy walked there. Then she saw she was not alone. Scarcely a block ahead, a silver-haired girl moved through the shadows and the neon glare from the Adults Only bookstores.

It was Jennie. And she was going somewhere. Cathy ran to catch up.

But no matter how fast she ran, Cathy was always behind, never gaining on Jennie's figure as she moved steadily through the Lower Basin. They threaded along deserted streets lined with pawn-shops and cheap hotels.

"Wait, Jennie!" Cathy called. "Wait for me!"

Jennie paused. Cathy got nearer. Then, when she was an arm's length away, the dim figure turned, and Cathy saw that it had no face—nothing under the honey-blond hair except a bloody skull. The bare jaws moved, and Jennie's voice came from between the fleshless rows of teeth.

"I've lost my legs," she said. "Please help me find them."

Cathy woke up in her bed, shivering and sweating at the same time. At first she had trouble moving, and she panicked before she realized that the clammy sheets had wrapped themselves around her body while she thrashed about in her nightmare. Slowly, she untangled herself and looked over at her digital alarm clock. The glowing scarlet numbers read 4:57.

"Was that when it happened, Jennie?" she whispered to the dark ceiling. "Is that what you're trying to tell me?"

No one answered.

Afraid to sleep again, Cathy lay awake until her window turned gray with the coming dawn. Then she dressed and went downstairs. She turned on the television to the local morning news.

No word on the Brodie murder, the announcer said, close to the end of the program. Cathy turned off the television, feeling depressed that Jennie's

34

death was already old news, even with an insane killer loose in the city and still no arrest. Cathy waited until her mother came down—her father was still on the road, probably headed home right now.

"Did you sleep all right, dear?" Mrs. Atmore asked anxiously.

"I'm okay," said Cathy. She didn't want to talk about her dream, or even remember it, now that she was awake. Mrs. Atmore frowned but said nothing, and mother and daughter shared a silent breakfast of Minute Oats before Cathy went off to school. Her breath steamed in the chilly air as she waited at the bus stop, and again as she walked from the bus to the school building.

It was Wednesday morning, halfway through the week. Her glasses fogged up as soon as she walked through the doors into the humid warmth of the lobby. She didn't bother taking them off to wipe her lenses; that seldom made things better. Instead, she let herself be guided by the blurry colored shapes around her in the hall and by her memory of the school layout.

Moving along with the people around her, she made her way toward her locker. Then, caught in a traffic jam of students, she heard a voice—Henry O'Toole telling another one of his crazy jokes.

"Did you hear," Henry said, "Don Fulman bought a new car?"

"No," said another voice. "Did he?"

"Yeah," said Henry. "And the dealer said, 'Are you sure you can afford it? This'll cost you an arm and a leg.' And Don said, 'No problem, I can get 'em.' "

Three or four people laughed, a hideous braying sound. Cathy's glasses blurred even more, and she felt tears trickling down her cheeks. She'd heard the rumors yesterday about what had happened, that Jennie's legs were missing and that the police hadn't found them. How could people laugh?

Without thinking, Cathy turned. She went back to the main door and walked out into the cold morning. Her glasses cleared as the dry air hit them.

Outside, the flow of kids into the building was slowing to a trickle as eight-thirty approached. Cathy turned and started walking toward downtown.

This was the first time she'd ever skipped school. She knew other kids who skipped, but mostly they were the sort whose parents didn't care, or who didn't care themselves what their parents thought. Her own mother would probably skin Cathy alive when she heard the news—and Mrs. Atmore was certain to hear it, since Cresswell High's main computer dialed the home phone number of every student reported absent from school and passed the word along. But right now, that didn't matter.

Cathy walked in the direction of the town's business district, where the office buildings and the expensive shops crowded close together. She tried not to bump into the business-people and secretaries on their way to nine-to-five jobs. Everyone was wearing the same outfit, like a uniform: a tailored suit in a subdued color under a beige London Fog trench coat. Cathy felt conspicuous wearing her school clothes and carrying her schoolbooks. At the bus station, near the divide between the business district and the Lower Basin, she found a pay locker. She put her books inside, put a quarter in the slot, and took the key. Now she was committed to staying away the whole day.

She wasn't going to go home, either. Not until she was ready. She didn't want to talk to her mother, didn't want to talk to anybody. She just wanted to think.

Cathy left the bus station and stood for a moment looking down toward the Lower Basin. The old factory district lay partly shrouded in a river fog that the morning sun hadn't burned away. Last night, in Cathy's dream, Jennie had walked those streets. Was the killer still down there? Or had he come from someplace else, like the Estates or Gaspee Farms? Did he have a familiar face? She shivered at the thought. Then, resolutely, she turned her back on the Basin and struck out for downtown.

The business district was depressing. One of the empty storefronts along Queen Street had a paper banner in the window. VOTE FOR BARBER FOR MAYOR! the sign proclaimed. VOTE FOR EFFECTIVE GOVERNMENT!

Todd Barber's father was a lawyer, Cathy remembered. He must be a candidate, then. She wondered what Todd's father was like and decided he was probably just like Todd, only older—always cool, always self-assured, always looking for exactly the right thing to say to make himself look good. A smooth mover, that was Todd.

Cathy had lunch in a little diner that served a Businessman's Special for three dollars and fifty cents. She felt out of place there, too, sitting in a corner booth at the back and afraid the whole time that someone who knew her would come in. But the only people she saw were secretaries.

The sky turned gray in the midafternoon. Low, dark clouds blew up out of the west, and the wind carried the prospect of freezing rain. Cathy browsed through the stores, staying long enough in each one to look over the merchandise and warm up, but not so long that anyone would notice her. She felt as if she had a big TRUANT sign pasted on her back.

When Cathy passed by the midtown video arcade and saw a bunch of boys in football jackets hunched over the joysticks, she knew school was over. She went back to the bus depot and collected her books. Then she thought about going home. Twilight would come in a couple of hours, and she didn't want to be caught out on the streets after dark.

But she still didn't want to go home. She couldn't face her mother, who by now surely knew that Cathy hadn't been in school. Mrs. Atmore probably had the police looking all over for her. Maybe not. Her mother hated to make a fuss. But there would still be a scene—"I was so worried about you, you gave me another gray hair." Cathy wasn't ready for that, not yet.

Instead, she headed in the direction of the Gaspee Farms housing development. Without really thinking, she let her feet carry her along the familiar route to Jennie's house. She didn't know what she was going to say when she got there; she just had a vague idea about knocking on the door and asking Mrs. Brodie if there was anything she could do to help.

She went up the neat sidewalk to a green-painted front door flanked by two holly bushes that produced red berries at Christmastime. Cathy remembered when Mr. Brodie had planted those bushes six summers before, the year after the Brodies had moved out of the Upper Basin. She and Jennie had helped, and Jennie had insisted on claiming one of the baby bushes for herself, and one for Cathy. It didn't seem right that both of the holly bushes should still be green and flourishing, now that Jennie was dead.

Cathy lifted the brass doorknocker and let it fall. Before she could knock again, the door swung open. A stranger stood inside—a man in a blue uniform, a policeman. Beyond him, she could see the wreckage of what had once been the Brodies' neat, pretty living room.

Someone had slashed open the bright chintz cushions on the overstuffed sofa and torn the pictures down off the wall. All the drawers in the rolltop desk had been pulled out and emptied onto the carpet. The big table lamp lay on the floor, its shade crushed and its porcelain base shattered.

Cathy felt sick, as if it were Jennie herself who was lying there broken, and not just a piece of furniture.

She swallowed hard and fought to get her voice under control. "What happened?" she asked.

The policeman didn't answer. "What's your name?"

She swallowed again. "Cathy Atmore."

"Come in, Miss Atmore."

Cathy went inside. She didn't want to, not with the house looking the way it did, but she didn't feel as if she had any choice. Inside, the Brodies' living room looked even worse. All the sheet music on the little upright piano had been ripped or crumpled, and the vandals had carved long deep gouges into the polished walnut veneer.

The policeman turned toward the back part of the house. "Hey, Detective!" he called. "Some kid named Atmore's here!"

A man in plainclothes walked out of the narrow hallway that led to the bedrooms.

"Miss Atmore," Detective Rogers said. He had a sheaf of computer paper in his hands.

He turned toward a man who wore a blue windbreaker with the words *Crime Lab* in white across the back. The other man was going over the furniture with something that looked like a fluffy paintbrush.

"It's okay," the other man said. "We got the prints from the kitchen already."

Rogers gestured toward the wooden chairs around

the table in the breakfast nook. "Miss Atmore," he said again. "Sit down."

Cathy sat down. Rogers didn't. He leaned forward over the table, both his hands flat on the blue-and-white-checked cloth, and he stood there looking down at her.

"Atmore," he said, "you're eighteen. That makes you an adult in the eyes of the law. I've got some questions for you, and you're going to answer them. You understand?"

Cathy felt ashamed, sitting here with a policeman talking to her as if she were some kind of criminal. *All I did was skip school.*

The detective was waiting for her to answer. Her throat felt tight, and she didn't know if she could talk without squeaking. She took a deep, shaky breath.

"Yes," she said. "I understand."

"Okay," Detective Rogers said. "Let's take it from the top. Where were you this morning?"

He already knows *I skipped school,* Cathy thought numbly. *What* else *does he want?* "What do you mean?"

The detective scowled. "Don't play dumb with me, Atmore. You weren't in school. Where were you?"

"I was just . . . walking around."

"Just walking around." The detective sounded as if he'd never heard of anybody doing that before. "Walking around where? Why?"

41

Cathy gave a helpless shrug. "I don't know." How could he expect her to explain what she'd been doing, when she didn't understand it herself? "I was just walking around downtown."

"Yeah? Anyone see you downtown?"

She thought about the secretaries, laughing together in the diner. "Not—not that I know."

"Where were you last Friday night?"

"I was at Eric's party, then I went home."

The detective's questions came faster now, and harder. She felt them hitting her, like rocks. "What time did you leave?"

He already knows this stuff. Why is he asking me all over again? "Nine or nine-thirty. I told you on Monday."

"You told me a lot of things," the detective said. "But I'll bet there are things you *didn't* tell me. And I'll bet some of the things you did tell me aren't true. Before we're done, you're going to tell me something that I'll believe."

"I told you the truth!" Cathy cried out.

But you didn't tell him everything, said the voice of her conscience. *You didn't tell him about how Jennie kept trying to tell you something, but Don kept getting in the way.*

Something must have shown in her face. The detective leaned forward, and his voice got a little louder.

"Listen, kid," he said. "I got a list here of everyone who was at that party. And I got another list here of everyone who wasn't at school today. You know what? You're the only one who's on both lists. I think there's a connection. And then today, while you were 'just walking around downtown,' this house gets broken into. How do you explain that?"

Cathy shook her head. "I can't."

"You'd better come up with an explanation that a judge'll believe," the detective told her. "And you'd better come up with it quick."

"Hey, wait a minute," Cathy said. Her voice sounded strange, high-pitched and shaky, and she could hear the blood rushing in her ears. "Do you think *I* did all this?"

"Did you?" asked the detective. "You were looking for her diary, weren't you? You didn't find it when you trashed the place this morning, so you came back again to look some more." Without warning, he leaned so far forward that his nose almost touched her glasses and snapped, "Where are Brodie's legs?"

"I don't know!" Cathy shouted back. Her body was starting to shake all over, and her stomach hurt. "Why are you asking me about that?"

"Because I think you *do* know," said the detective. "I think you know who cut off Jennie Brodie's legs, and I think you know where they are right now."

"*I do not!*" Cathy screamed at him. "I do not, I do not, I do not!"

The force of her own unaccustomed anger choked her, and she began to cry—long, racking sobs that

43

tore and clawed their way out of her chest and into her throat.

"Come on," Detective Rogers said. "We're taking a little ride downtown."

Chapter 5

At the police station, Detective Rogers's questioning went on. He kept making Cathy repeat her story —where she'd gone when she cut school that day, whom she'd seen on the night of Eric's party, what she'd done over the weekend.

Over and over, he asked her the same questions, sometimes worded in one way, sometimes in another, but always the same, and always coming back to the one question that Cathy didn't have any answer for at all: what had happened to Jennie's missing legs?

The cops hadn't told anybody about that, but the whole high school was talking about it anyway. Somebody at Cresswell knew more than they should. Was it her?

Cathy lost track of time. She couldn't keep straight which things she'd told Detective Rogers during her first interview and which ones she'd forgotten until too late. She couldn't even remember whether she'd called home yet, or whether she'd just been wanting to for so long that she'd imagined it.

Finally, when she was so tired that she could only

nod her head mutely yes and no to the detective's questions, she heard a heavy tread in the corridor outside. Detective Rogers looked past her shoulder at the door.

"Mr. Atmore," he said.

Cathy turned in her chair and saw her father coming into the room. He still had on the heavy boots and the red-and-black wool jacket that he wore out on the road. His eyes were red-rimmed and weary, and he needed a shave.

He must have come over to the station as soon as he got back into town. Heaped on top of everything else, the realization was just too much; Cathy started crying again, and this time she couldn't stop.

"Oh, Daddy," she wailed between sobs. "I'm sorry, I'm so sorry! I didn't mean to make any trouble."

Mr. Atmore laid a warm hand on her shoulder. "Everything's all right, honey." He turned to Detective Rogers. "I've come to take my daughter home."

The detective didn't argue. "I have no further questions at this time," he said. "But I advise her not to leave town."

Cathy's father drove her home in his pickup—a five-year-old Chevy with a gun rack in the rear window. Cathy was still sobbing. For a long time they didn't speak. Finally Mr. Atmore broke the silence.

"Your mom's pretty upset. Skipping school, and then this."

Cathy drew a deep, gulping breath. "I didn't mean to get in trouble, honest. It was just—people kept talking about Jennie, and they wouldn't shut up. I had to get away."

"Doesn't look like it worked."

She sniffled. "I know."

Her father glanced over at her. "Tell me straight, Cath. Are you mixed up in this mess, or are the cops just giving you a hard time?"

"Some of both, I think," she admitted, after another long silence. "They've been talking to everybody—but I was Jennie's best friend, and I think she wanted to tell me something last Friday night at Eric's party. Maybe to the police I look guilty, I don't know."

"They're leaning on you," said her father. "They think you know something you won't tell, and they want to push you into talking. They better be careful they don't lean too hard."

He pulled up outside the house in the Upper Basin. "Here we are," he said. "Let's go in and get it over with."

The next half hour wasn't pleasant. Cathy's grilling from the police had felt like nothing compared to the one she got from her mother, which included a question Detective Rogers had never thought to ask: "How could you do this to us?"

Eventually, though, the accusations and reproaches ended, and Cathy was able to stumble upstairs to bed, too upset to eat dinner. And tonight, at least, she was too tired and wrung-out to dream, or to remember it if she did.

The next morning, her father drove her to school

and promised to come back for her that afternoon. He didn't say anything, but she knew he was making sure she didn't cut school again.

At school, things weren't any better than they had been the day before. In fact, they were worse. Everywhere she went, there were sidelong glances, meaningful nods and pointed fingers, whispers that stopped when she entered a room and started again when she left. No one would talk to her directly, not even people she'd thought were her friends. It was as if she'd developed a horrible skin disease, and everybody thought it might be catching.

Don't worry, she thought bitterly after the third or fourth snub in as many minutes. *I've got a little case of "murder suspect." There's a lot of that going around.*

She was tired, too, after yesterday's wandering downtown, followed by Detective Rogers's questions at the police station and the emotional scene at home. She had trouble staying awake in her classes, and when she glimpsed her reflection by accident in a pane of glass, she almost didn't recognize the pale, swollen-eyed girl who stared back out at her.

No wonder Don Fulman had looked bad on Tuesday, if the police had put him through the same wringer the night before. Not that Cathy felt all that sympathetic. Not even being a murder suspect had gotten Don kicked out of his place in Cresswell High's top crowd—no case of invisible leprosy for him.

It must be because he was Don Fulman before all this

happened, and he's still Don Fulman. But I was just Jennie's friend, and now there's no more Jennie.

At lunch, Don ate his usual hamburger at the group's usual table, but Cathy couldn't find a seat even though she got there early. All the empties turned out to be saved for other people. She wound up sitting at the next table over, where the wannabee cheerleaders and the second-string jocks sat to be close to their idols. Nobody talked to her at that table, either.

When she left, Don stood up at the same time and walked out of the room after her. He loomed over Cathy and spoke in a low voice. "If you talk to the cops, you're dog meat."

Don was big and broad-shouldered, and he could be violent sometimes. Everybody at Cresswell knew about his aggressive playing style on the football field and about those episodes off of it when his temper cut loose and exploded into physical action—like that fight with Len Pelsher.

Maybe he's crazy, maybe he really did kill Jennie, and now he's threatening to kill me. The thought made Cathy's hands shake and her mouth feel stiff. But she forced herself to look straight back at Don, even though she knew the thick lenses of her glasses made her look dizzy and goggle-eyed instead of strong and unintimidated.

"You mean, dead?" she asked. "Like Jennie?"

He scowled down at her. "You're supposed to be so smart, *you* figure it out. But if you're going to make a choice, you'd better hurry."

Then he went back into the cafeteria, leaving Cathy blinking in the hall as she tried to puzzle out his meaning. Was Don trying to threaten her into keeping secret something she wasn't even aware she knew, something that would mark him as the murderer? Or did he, too, suspect Cathy of killing Jennie? Or could it be a warning?

It wasn't as if the cops had forgotten Don in their eagerness to grill Cathy. Last night's ordeal at the police station had given painful evidence of that fact. Detective Rogers had asked almost as many questions about Don Fulman as he had about Jennifer Brodie.

Thinking about some of those questions still made Cathy feel sick. *What kind of relationship did Jennie have with Don? Had she gone all the way with him? What kind of relationship did Don have with you? Did he go all the way with you? Was Don afraid that Jennie would find out about you and him? What do you mean, there wasn't anything between you and Don? Then why does everyone remember you hanging around with Don all the time?*

And on and on, for what felt like forever.

The school day, too, seemed to drag on interminably. By the time classes ended in the afternoon, Cathy had gotten the cold shoulder so many times from so many different people that she'd lost count. When Stu Martin came up in the hallway and started a conversation with her, she almost felt grateful. Stu might possess the social skills of a third grader, but at least he didn't act as if she had something contagious.

"Hey, Cathy," he said. "How's it going?"

She looked at him and wondered if he really hadn't noticed that everybody else had started pulling away from her as soon as word got out she was a suspect.

"Everything's going okay," she said, "unless you count having the cops think I teamed up with Don Fulman to kill Jennie because of some kind of love triangle."

He blinked at her. His glasses were almost as thick as hers. "That could be uncomfortable," he said. "Did you?"

"No, I did not," she said wearily. You couldn't resent Stu; you just had to take him on his own terms. He was brilliant—but on the day they passed out empathy, he'd been hiding behind the door. "And I don't know what makes the police think I did, either."

"It's a pretty reasonable thing to think," Stu said, "if you're dumb enough to be a cop."

"Not you, too!" she said. "I can't take this any longer."

Cathy turned away in the direction of her locker. *At least I don't have to worry about hurting Stu's feelings. He hasn't got any.*

She walked off. But when she reached the corner where two of the school's main hallways crossed, she paused and glanced back. She half-expected to see Stu standing there looking nonplussed—but some-

51

what to her surprise he was talking to Pam Greeley, who was the head cheerleader now that Jennie was gone. Oddly enough, it looked as if Pam had come up to Stu, rather than the other way around. Their voices carried to her in the empty corridor.

"I have to have it," Pam was saying, a panicky sound in her voice. "Can you tell him I need it?"

"I can pass the word along," Stu said. "But this stuff takes time."

"That's not good enough," Pam said. It sounded as if she were going to start crying. "I need it now—today."

"I'll see what I can do," Stu said.

"You can find me—" Pam began, but she cut off short as her head swung around. She froze when she saw Cathy, then she walked away quickly.

Cathy watched her for a moment, then walked back over to Stu. "What did *she* want?" Cathy asked.

He shrugged. "Same thing as all the other jocks and cheerleaders want," he said. "I have what they need."

"What's that?"

He paused for a moment before replying. "I'm smarter than they are," he told her. "They want help with their homework and things like that. Most of them can't add two and two without counting on their fingers first."

"Well, I can," said Cathy. "What you're talking about is cheating."

Stu looked at her through his thick glasses and

didn't say anything. Cathy got a creepy feeling down her back.

"It isn't just the homework, is it?" she said quietly. Then she turned her back on him and went to her locker.

She took out her key, unlocked the padlock, and pulled open the door. Inside, her coat hung from one of the two metal hooks on the locker's rear wall.

She took out the coat and began to put it on. She had one arm up a sleeve and the other one groping for an armhole when she saw it—something pale lying on the bottom of the locker. A plastic fashion doll in a cheerleader's uniform, with long honey-blond hair just like Jennie's.

Cathy picked up the doll. It had a strip of black tape over its mouth. And its legs were missing.

Chapter 6

Cathy slammed her locker shut on the gagged and mutilated doll. For a moment she stood with her hand on the door handle, trembling all over and breathing hard. She looked up and down the hall. Pam and Stu had both vanished. Nobody else was in sight except for one of the school custodians pushing a broom far away at the end of the hall.

She opened her locker again. The doll was still there.

Slowly, stiffly, she bent down and picked the doll up. *Throw it away, Cath. Get rid of it before somebody sees you holding it.*

She looked around for a trash can. Down by the lobby? No good—the custodian was heading that way now. He might see her throw the doll away, and think—who knew what he might think? He would know as much gossip as everybody else did, if not more. There are no secrets from school custodians.

Cathy stuffed the doll inside her book bag and shut her locker. Maybe she could use the dumpster out in the parking lot, as long as nobody was around.

But the dumpster idea was no good, either. The horn of her father's pickup honked twice, loudly, as soon as she stepped out through the front door of Cresswell High, and she had to go straight over and climb into the cab.

"How was your day?" her father asked as he pulled the pickup away from the curb. "Anybody give you any trouble?"

Cathy shrugged. "Nothing I shouldn't have expected. I'm still alive."

As she spoke, she was aware of the hard plastic lump of the doll inside her book bag. She wanted to tell her father about finding it, but telling him would be the same as telling her mother, and then there would be more emotional scenes.

If Mom ever sees that doll, she'll be down at the police station telling them that the killer left it in my locker and that I'm his next target.

Cathy shivered. Her mother could be right. But Cathy still didn't feel like listening to her go on and on about it. Not until she'd had a chance to unwind a bit first.

After dinner would be the best time. She would show the doll to her parents then.

She went upstairs as soon as she got home. She pulled the mutilated doll out of her book bag and thrust it into the bottom drawer of her desk. Then she took out her notebook and started to do her homework. One good thing about being in the doghouse at school and at home, Cathy reflected—she was going to get a lot of studying done.

She was working on her math when the phone rang down in the living room. Her mother called up the stairs, "Cathy, honey, it's for you."

Cathy walked downstairs as slowly as she dared. What if it was the police on the other end of the line, or a call from whoever had left that hideous message in her locker? But it was only Cheryl Barkham.

"Hey, Cath," Cheryl said, "I just want you to know that I feel really bad about how everybody is treating you at school. It's horrible. I know you didn't have anything to do with what happened to Jennie."

"Thanks," Cathy said without enthusiasm. If Cheryl had felt all that bad, she could have come over and sat with Cathy at lunch. "I appreciate that."

"But did you hear the latest?" Cheryl asked.

She was just eager to pass on the gossip, Cathy realized. Cheryl ought to try being the object of gossip for a little while—it would give her a whole different perspective.

"No," Cathy said aloud. "I didn't hear."

"It happened yesterday while you were gone. Some kid, a sophomore, fell down in the hall."

"So what's strange about that?" Cathy asked. "The way they wax the floors, you could go skating in there sometimes."

"Yeah—but after he was on the floor, he started ripping at his clothes and yelling, 'The bugs, oh, no, the bugs! Get 'em off me!' Men in white coats took him away in an ambulance, and nobody's seen him since."

"Weird," said Cathy, since some kind of reply seemed to be in order. "I feel like doing that myself sometimes, like after one of Osgood's history classes."

Cheryl gave a polite laugh at the other end of the line. "Listen, Cath, I've got to run. Talk with you tomorrow, okay?"

"Okay. 'Bye."

Cathy hung up the phone and sat waiting for it to ring again. Who was going to look for thrills by calling her next? She was still looking at the phone when a knock sounded at the door.

She hurried to answer the knock, leaving the chain on as she opened the door a crack. Detective Rogers stood on the front step.

"Good afternoon, Miss Atmore," he said. "May I come in?"

"You'll have to talk to my father," she said. "Wait a minute while I tell him you're here."

She closed the door again and went into the kitchen, where her mother was fixing a meatloaf for dinner and her father sat at the table drinking coffee.

"Dad," she said, "that police detective is here. He wants to talk to you."

Mr. Atmore set down his mug of coffee and went out of the room. There was a rumble of voices—the detective's, her father's, the detective's again—and then Mr. Atmore came back into the kitchen. Detective Rogers came with him.

"He has a warrant," Cathy's father told her.

"I'm looking for certain articles of clothing, bloodstains, knives, that kind of thing," the detective said. "It's all in the warrant." He tossed a sheaf of paper—about seventy-five pages' worth—onto the blue-and-white-checked tablecloth. "No one is to leave this room."

"Before you start," Mr. Atmore said, "I'd better tell you. There's a weapon in the front hall closet."

"What kind?" Rogers asked.

"A shotgun. I use it for deer hunting."

"Right," said the detective. "A shotgun isn't alleged in the warrant. Do you have all your receipts and licenses?"

"Sure. You want me to go get them?"

"Yes." The detective nodded to one of his men. "Go with him."

They went out together, and Mr. Atmore came back a few minutes later to sit down again with Mrs. Atmore and Cathy. More police officers came, until the house overflowed with men and women in blue uniforms. They did a very thorough job, tramping up and down the stairs from attic to basement, opening and shutting cupboards and drawers and closets. Cathy and her parents sat in uncomfortable silence at the kitchen table and waited for them to finish.

After what felt like hours, Detective Rogers came back into the kitchen carrying a plastic bag sealed with a strip of red tape. The tape had the word EVI-

DENCE printed on it in white. He tossed the bag onto the table on top of the warrant.

Cathy looked at the plastic bag, at the gagged and legless doll sealed up inside it.

"All right," said Detective Rogers. "Are you going to tell me about this or not?"

"It's not mine," said Cathy. "I found it this afternoon in my locker at school."

The detective frowned. "Then why was it hidden in your desk upstairs?"

"I didn't hide it," said Cathy. "I just . . . put it there after I brought it home."

"You say you found the doll in your locker," said the detective. "Can you tell me who might have left it there?"

Cathy could only shake her head. "I don't know. But it isn't mine."

"Sure it isn't," said Rogers. His expression had changed—the discovery of the legless doll seemed to have helped him make up his mind about something.

"You have the right to remain silent," he told Cathy. "You have the right to consult an attorney. If you do not have an attorney, a public defender will be appointed for you free of charge. Any statement you make may be used against you in the event of a trial at law. Do you understand these rights as I have explained them to you?"

Unable to speak, Cathy nodded. *He's reading me my rights. He really thinks that I murdered my best friend and cut off her legs.*

Before the detective could say anything further, however, a uniformed officer came into the kitchen. "Detective Rogers," he said, "call for you, sir."

"I'll be right back," the detective said, and he left the room.

He returned in only a couple of minutes. "We're done here," he said to policemen gathered around. Then he turned to Cathy.

"Okay," Rogers said. "I'm not arresting you—yet. Just don't leave town, and don't do anything stupid."

He gathered up the warrant and the broken doll in its plastic nest and walked to the kitchen door. He paused on the threshold. "By the way, if you remember anything you forgot to mention, call me up. Any time, day or night. It could save you a lot of grief."

Then he was gone. Cathy's mother and father sat looking at her for a moment without saying anything. Finally her mother said, "You didn't really"— Mrs. Atmore paused uneasily, groping for the right words—"really *do* anything, did you, dear?"

"Mom—no," Cathy said faintly.

"Of course she didn't," said her father, cutting off Cathy's reply. "They think she knows something, and they're trying to put on some pressure, that's all."

"But this is America," protested her mother. "The police can't just barge into people's homes without a reason!"

"They can always get a reason when they need one," said Mr. Atmore. "All they need is a dime to call a judge, any judge, and convince him that some anonymous tipster said there was evidence of some crime at some location. That's all it takes. And then they can go fishing."

A tipster. Someone who knew I took the doll home. Maybe the custodian saw me with it after all.

"They don't have a case against anyone," Mr. Atmore reassured his wife. "If they had a case, they'd have made an arrest. All they have is smoke, and they're shifting it with their hands as fast as they can."

The red light on the Madsens' telephone answering machine was blinking steadily when Bill brought his mother home from work late in the afternoon.

"Check out the message, will you, Bill?" she asked as she hung up her coat in the front hall closet. The day had turned suddenly warm about noon, after a cold snap that had lasted since the previous Friday, and she'd ended up carrying the coat rather than wearing it.

Bill pushed the playback button. The machine beeped once, and a rough voice said, *"Doctor Madsen? This is the A. J. Borden Garage and Auto-body Shop. It's Thursday, nine-thirty A.M. Your Saab is ready to go."*

"Oh, good," Dr. Madsen said as the machine beeped twice and started rewinding the tape. "I'll be happy to have my own car back. You know I hate imposing on you like this."

"It's okay, Mom," Bill said. "No real hassle. You

want to go get it? I can drive you down to the garage right now, before they close."

They drove back to the garage, a small, rather grubby-looking business in the old part of town. But Dr. Madsen didn't believe in judging things by surface appearances; she'd done too many autopsies for that. What counted with her was the Borden Garage's high reputation among local car owners for honesty and reliability, and a mechanic who really understood Saabs.

Bill pulled up in front of the garage, and Dr. Madsen got out. "This shouldn't take more than a couple of minutes," she said. "But you'd better stick around until we're sure it actually runs."

She went on into the shop, and Bill parked the Ford. He thought about waiting outside but decided that just sitting around in the car would be even more boring than going inside and waiting there. He locked up the car and joined his mother in the shop's tiny, cluttered office. His mother was just finishing up the paperwork.

"There you go," said the mechanic. He nodded toward where one of the garage's big main doors opened onto a lot filled with parked cars. "I'll help you find it outside. Put it there this morning."

"Thank you," said Dr. Madsen. She walked out of the garage toward the car. Bill drifted along after them.

A few feet away from the Saab, Dr. Madsen paused. Her nostrils twitched faintly, and a furrow appeared between her eyebrows. She sniffed again, more deliberately.

"What is it, Mom?" Bill asked.

"I'm not sure," she replied, but Bill recognized the note in her voice. His mother was sure, all right; she just didn't want to say something before it was time.

Lips compressed, Dr. Madsen walked slowly around the Saab. Then she zeroed in on the trunk. Bill moved closer as well. There *was* an odor, Bill thought, a faint one, as if there were a very old cheese lying around. Limburger, maybe.

"What's that stink?" he asked.

"Maybe it's coolant," his mother replied. She didn't sound as if she really thought it was.

The mechanic shook his head. "There was nothing wrong with your cooling system," he said. "Maybe you forgot and left some groceries or something in the trunk. It's been freezing all week until today—everything would have kept just fine until the weather started warming up."

"Let's have a look," said Dr. Madsen grimly. She pulled her keyring from her purse, picked out a key, and inserted it into the trunk lock. She turned the key.

The trunk opened, and a wave of heavy odor came rolling out. Inside the trunk, Bill saw a clear plastic sheet, wrapped around something long and dark and wet-looking. Dr. Madsen took a step forward and wrinkled her nose.

"Get back, Bill," she said. "And go call the police."

The mechanic stepped up to the trunk, holding his hand over his nose. Then abruptly he was sick, the contents of his stomach spewing over the rear bumper of the car and dribbling down onto his shoes.

Bill stayed at the garage while he waited for the police. When Detective Rogers finally came, he questioned Bill, in a great deal of detail, as to why Jennie Brodie's legs might have been hidden in his mother's car, a car to which only Bill had access at the time when Jennie Brodie died.

Chapter 7

The morning after Detective Rogers's visit, Cathy found herself back in class. She'd wanted to stay home, but her father had said, "Don't give 'em any reason to talk about you," and he insisted that she finish her cornflakes and get into the pickup.

Once Cathy got to school, she didn't bother trying to start conversations with the other students. If she kept to herself, nobody would have a chance to snub her.

Between classes, she watched Don Fulman. Usually, by this time on a Friday morning, he'd be sitting up on the auditorium stage with the rest of the team while the band played the Cresswell fight song and Jennie led the student body in cheers. But Jennie was dead, and the regular Friday pep rally had been canceled. Instead of listening to the roar of the crowd, Don stalked through the halls with a scowl on his face, ignoring the football groupies trailing in his wake.

She was beginning to wonder about Don. Just because the cops talk to you, she reflected as the lockers banged open and shut around her, doesn't make you guilty. And in spite of his nasty temper, Don had never done Jennie any actual harm.

As for his threat the day before—she could understand that now. She might threaten someone herself, considering the mood she was in. No one in the school would talk to her.

Stu Martin emerged out of the press of students hurrying from class to class. "Hi, Cathy. How are you doing today?"

Correction. One person will talk to me. The chief nerd of Nerd Central.

Then she felt guilty about her thought. Stu couldn't help being the way he was, and for that matter, she knew how she herself looked to the jocks and cheerleaders: a nerd like Stu, female variety.

"Hi, Stu," she said. "I'm in a bit of a rush right now."

"Can we talk later?"

"Uh, probably. But I really have to get to class. I'll see you at the Hackers' Club after school."

Cathy went on to her next class. Cheryl Barkham arrived a minute or so later and sat down in her usual place.

Cheryl leaned across the aisle. "Have you heard the latest?" she whispered.

"Probably not," said Cathy truthfully. *Not even Cheryl would be so eager to spread gossip that she'd tell me about the cops searching my own house!* "What happened?"

"The cops arrested Bill Madsen last night,"

Cheryl told her. "I heard it from my brother, who works downtown near the police station."

Cathy frowned. Compared to someone like Don Fulman, Bill made a strangely unconvincing brutal killer. True, he did live right next to the place where Jennie was last seen alive, and true, he was kind of a creep. But if that was enough to make someone a murderer, Cathy should be in handcuffs, too.

Then she remembered Detective Rogers's "Don't leave town." She might be closer than she knew to being arrested.

Not until lunch hour did the students at Cresswell get the full story of Bill Madsen's arrest. Martin Feldman, who kept a Walkman in his locker to listen to the sports reports during lunch, heard about it on *Noontime Newsbreak.* Within minutes, everybody in the cafeteria knew that Jennifer Brodie's missing legs had turned up in the trunk of Dr. Elizabeth Madsen's Saab.

Henry O'Toole, of course, was in his element. "I've heard of carrying spare parts," he said to his usual audience, "but this is ridiculous." He paused. "I guess Bill finally swept a girl off her feet." Another pause; this time, he got a few bursts of nervous, guilty laughter out of his uneasy audience. "So anyway, the cops won't have to do any more legwork."

Henry did a quick drum-roll on the table with his fingers to mark the final punchline.

"O'Toole, you really are sick," someone said.

"Yeah," Henry agreed. "But see how much fun I have?"

Cathy poked at her salad with her fork and tried to shut out the conversation. She was back in her old spot at the table. It looked as if Bill's arrest had taken both herself and Don off the hook as far as public opinion went.

She glanced over at Don, trying not to stare. Jennie's boyfriend still looked as if he hadn't been getting enough sleep. He was pale and had dark circles under his eyes.

Pretty much how I'd look if these glasses didn't hide two-thirds of my face.

She poked again at her salad. Today's lunch hour was dragging out even longer than yesterday's. She had her old place back, but without Jennie around, nobody bothered to talk to her, and she had nothing to block her ears against Henry O'Toole's sick jokes coming from two tables over.

After a few more minutes, she laid down her fork and sat back, quietly thinking. Maybe it was because she'd been speculating about Don Fulman and Bill Madsen and the different ways people behaved; or maybe it was just because she was stuck here at the popular students' table with nothing to do but watch people come and go. But she noticed something interesting.

When jocks and cheerleaders left their tables, they didn't always head for obvious places like the line for seconds or the water fountain. In fact, there was a regular pattern of circulation during lunch. One by one students from that clique would get up and leave the cafeteria—not for the rest room, either; they left by the wrong door for that—and then they would return.

Cathy had never noticed the pattern before today. She'd always been interested in the people who *were* there, not the people who weren't. Maybe it was time she changed that around.

Cathy got up and went to the water fountain herself. Then she waited for another student from the popular table to leave the cafeteria. When Mark Metzger, the second-string tight end, got up and went out the same door as all the others, Cathy followed. To her surprise, Mark strode purposefully through the halls and downstairs to the computer lab.

Cathy paused at the bottom of the steps and stared at the closed door. This was where the most fashionable kids in the school were sneaking off to? She stood in the hall for a moment, undecided, then shrugged. What the heck—she was a regular member of the Hackers' Club; she could go into the computer lab during lunch hour.

"They can't think that. He'd have to be nuts to hide the legs in his mom's car," she heard someone saying as she opened the door.

And another voice said, "Yeah—but they probably figure a person would have to be nuts to kill someone anyway."

Cathy went on into the lab. The two speakers were Mark Metzger and Stu Martin. As soon as Mark caught sight of Cathy, he stopped talking, turned, and hurried out.

69

Stu looked at her in what might have been irritation. "What are you doing here?"

"I'm a member, too," she replied. "I can use the lab between classes if I like."

Then, because she was feeling a little overbearing and Stu was about the only person she could bear over, she added, "I don't think it's nice spreading stories about people. You don't know if they're true. Bill is supposed to be your friend."

Stu sat down in front of his usual computer. He spoke to the CRT screen without turning around. "I'd be careful, if I were you," he said. "Not everything or everyone is what they seem. People get hurt sometimes."

"What do you mean by that?"

He turned and looked directly at her. "Why don't you go back to lunch?"

Cathy was surprised by the vehement tone. *Maybe he really is worried about Bill after all.*

The next morning, Saturday, was Jennie's funeral —the coroner's department had finally released her body the night before. The brief warm spell of the last two days had ended, and a cold mist drifted across the cemetery plots. Rain had been falling off and on all morning, though not steadily or heavily enough for anyone to open an umbrella.

Cathy wore a dark blue dress, the closest she could come to black in her wardrobe. Even if the family could afford it, she wasn't going to buy a black dress just for funerals. She didn't plan on going to any more of them.

The Brodies' parish priest spoke about the hope of rising again. Cathy felt relieved that at least now Jennie was going to be able to rise with her legs attached. She hoped that Jennie's legs had been placed into the casket after the police were finished with them. She couldn't know for sure; it was a closed-casket funeral. According to all the hot rumors—rumors that Cheryl said Bill Madsen had started—there hadn't been much left of Jennie's face.

More people came to Jennie's funeral than Cathy had expected, even with Jennie as popular as she'd been. Mr. and Mrs. Brodie had come back from Boston, of course, where they'd been staying with Jennie's grandparents to get away from the reporters and gossip in Cresswell. All the cheerleaders and the football players were standing close together at the front of the crowd—Pam and Stacy looking stylish in their dark dresses, and the jocks looking uncomfortable in their suits.

Detective Rogers and a couple of his people had also come. The police officers stood a little apart from the rest of the mourners, watching who came and who went. Exactly why the cops were there, Cathy couldn't decide. Maybe police had feelings, too, and they wanted to bid farewell to someone whom they had—in their own way—gotten to know. Cathy hoped that was the reason, but looking at the hard expression in Rogers's eyes, somehow she doubted it.

Were they watching to see if someone came to the funeral, a stranger, someone who didn't fit? Could that mean that Bill hadn't acted alone—or, worse yet, that the police still weren't sure Bill was the right suspect? She looked quickly away from them, afraid they'd notice her.

She watched as Jennie's coffin was lowered into the grave. The straps of the machinery made a whirring sound. Nearby, a pile of dirt waited under a carpet of phony grass.

Don Fulman stood at the graveside, looking down at the polished coffin. He stood alone—no one seemed willing to get close to him, probably because Jennie's boyfriend looked as if he were half-crazy. People pretended not to see him, like they pretended not to see that pile of dirt.

The first symbolic handfuls of soil thumped down into the grave. The clods fell with muffled thuds upon the polished coffin.

With that sound, Don's lips moved. He spoke aloud, although he may not have realized it—loud enough so that Cathy heard.

"I did it," he muttered. "I killed her."

Cathy looked up, startled. Don's eyes were deep-set, staring fixedly at the grave in front of him. She wasn't sure he realized he'd spoken, or understood what he had said.

She thought she might have imagined the words, except for one thing: when she looked away, she saw Todd Barber standing with the rest of his family among the mourners. Todd's face had the expression of someone who had just been hit with a brick. He'd heard Don say those words, too.

That night, Cathy dreamed again.

This time, in her dream, she stood once more in the graveyard where Jennie was buried. Grass had sprouted from the grave, under the tombstone that read JENNIFER MARIE BRODIE, BELOVED DAUGHTER. THE MAIDEN IS NOT DEAD, BUT SLEEPETH.

Cathy looked about and saw that the season was no longer autumn, but early springtime. In the purple shadows beneath the trees, little patches of snow lay still unmelted. Only a few feet away, in the sunlight, yellow and white crocuses bloomed.

Abruptly, the landscape wavered and changed— from the springtime cemetery to the bare trees and brown, withered grass of Johnson's Swamp. Ragged clouds scudded by overhead on a cold autumn wind, just as they had on that day when the hunters had found Jennie's body.

Then, from beyond the trees, Cathy heard a girl's voice, screaming and sobbing. Between the cries and sobs came the same words repeated over and over: *"Oh, no, help me! Help me!"*

It was Jennie's voice. Cathy stood, frozen, while the screaming died away. After a long-drawn-out, silent pause, the bushes under the trees began to shake and rustle, as if some big clumsy animal were trying to move through them.

Then the thing emerged, and Cathy began to scream herself.

* * *

Cathy awoke with a start. She was still in her own room, and it was dark. Her heart was pounding frighteningly hard.

"Oh, Jennie, Jennie," she whispered. "I haven't forgotten you!"

She collapsed again onto her sweat-soaked pillow. But she didn't get back to sleep that night, because the last image from her nightmare had burned itself permanently into Cathy's brain: Jennifer Brodie, legless and blood-spattered, dragging herself out of the bushes by her arms.

And she didn't have a face.

Chapter 8

Cathy stayed indoors all day Sunday, reading and rereading the newspaper accounts of Jennie's murder and Bill Madsen's arrest. The papers didn't have anything at all to say about Don Fulman, and she wondered if the police had forgotten about him.

She still had the card with Detective Rogers's number on it. More than once that Sunday, she took it out and went to the telephone. But each time she put the card back into her purse, uncertain whether telling the detective about Don's mumblings at the funeral would do anyone any good. Rogers hadn't done anything to make Cathy either like or trust him. And besides, if the police hadn't had enough evidence to arrest Don before, what could they do with him now?

Monday morning she was back at school, with the card still in her purse and the phone number still undialed. Don Fulman was also back in school, looking more nervous than usual, and less rested. Jennie's boyfriend seemed to have lost ten pounds in the last week. His face, always thin, looked gaunt and ill.

He seemed to be avoiding Cathy, much as everyone else was avoiding him. Cathy heard the whispers —sitting next to Cheryl in class, she could hardly avoid them—that Don had gone nuts, that he'd flipped out from grief. People stay away from crazy people, and Don was crazy. Was he the one? Did he murder Jennie, like he said? And if the cops really did have the killer, then why was Jennie still appearing in her dreams?

She thought about the question all during homeroom. She didn't believe in ghosts, not really—but what if the dreams did mean something?

Even if they're just my own subconscious mind talking to me, if they're pointing at something I ought to do, then I should pay attention. If only I knew more. . . .

She would have to find out more—even if it meant asking Don point-blank what he'd meant when he'd said at the funeral that he'd killed Jennie.

Getting close enough to Don Fulman to ask him anything, however, turned out to be harder than Cathy had expected. He wasn't in many of her classes; in fact, except for study hall, the only time she saw him regularly was at lunch. And today, even that failed.

After waiting without result for almost the whole lunch period, Cathy gave up. She threw her half-eaten sandwich into the organic-trash bin, put the empty plate and the tray onto the conveyor belt running back into the kitchen, and left the cafeteria for the computer lab.

Don probably wouldn't be in the lab, either. He

was no computer expert, and he didn't need to hang around with the geeky types that were. On the other hand, Cathy still hadn't figured out what even a second-string jock like Mark Metzger had been doing down in the lab last week. Something decidedly odd was going on between the athletic set and the Hackers' Club.

At the door of the computer lab, she paused. People were talking in there again—she could hear their voices all the way out in the corridor.

"I can tell when someone's been messing with the system," one voice said. She wasn't certain who the speaker was, except that he was one of the Hackers' Club regulars. "And I don't think it's a good idea."

The second voice, however, she recognized at once as Stu Martin's. "As long as nobody gets caught, what's the problem?"

"The administration might find out, that's what," said the other voice. "And they'll think of us, first thing. Maybe we'll lose our machine privileges. I'd hate to get kicked out of here for something I didn't do. Whoever's messing with the machines isn't as clever as he thinks he is. I'd never turn in another hacker—"

"Definitely not a good idea," agreed Stu.

"—but if the system locks up again, or any more data turns up missing, I'll find out why."

Cathy opened the door, and Stu Martin and Larry Davidson turned around at the noise. She glanced at Larry—the club's youngest member was a sophomore who'd skipped a couple of grades in elementary school, and he almost never spoke up around the older members. For Larry to actually challenge a senior like Stu Martin, whatever he'd noticed going on in the system must have been serious.

Both Stu and Larry quit talking as soon as Cathy came in, and neither one said anything to her. *Oh, well. If there's something funny going on with the system, I'll probably notice it, too.*

She waited, and after a while Larry left, followed by Stu. When they were gone, Cathy booted her computer and checked the Cresswell High electronic bulletin board for E-mail messages.

"Letter waiting? YES," said the glowing green letters on the CRT screen. *"Read letter?"*

"YES," she typed.

The screen cleared, and the new message scrolled into view. Three words, no more:

"ATMORE, YOU'RE NEXT."

The message scrolled up to the top of the screen and then vanished. Cathy sat back in her chair, stunned. Did this mean that the Hackers' Club was involved in Jennie's murder? The idea seemed impossible—Jennie had stayed as far away from the computer lab as you could and still expect to graduate from Cresswell High. On the other hand, Cathy realized with a shiver, Bill Madsen was an active member of the club.

But he's not in school right now, she reminded herself. *The police have him.* Then she thought of something else. *If he's out on bail, maybe he could have gotten*

78

into the school's bulletin board system from his home computer. Maybe that's how we got the stuff Larry was complaining about.

She tried to call up the mysterious message again, intending to spend some time checking it out further, but it had already erased itself. She looked for the copy that should have been stored in the bulletin board archives and found none.

Cathy considered that. Whoever had left the message was good, really good, with computers, to make it disappear like that, leaving no trace behind in the system. That seemed to rule out Don Fulman. Bill, on the other hand, actually was that good.

The message itself, she realized, could be read two ways, either as a threat from an enemy or as a warning from a friend. She'd gotten that kind of mixed signal once before, and that time it *had* been from Don Fulman, speaking to her face-to-face: *"If you talk to the cops, you're dog meat."*

The bell that ended the lunch hour rang while Cathy was still staring at the blank screen of her computer. She shut down the terminal. Time to get to her next class. And, more desperately, time to find and talk with Don.

Cathy finally caught up with Don Fulman by sprinting from her last class as soon as the last bell rang and hanging around his locker. A minute or so later, he showed up to yank open his locker, throw in his textbooks, and take his letter jacket off the hook in back. She stepped forward out of the rush of departing students.

"Don," she began, "we have to talk."

He stopped with one arm halfway up a jacket sleeve. "I don't have anything to say to you."

Cathy flinched at his angry voice and at the way his eyes glittered under their heavy black brows. Nevertheless, she struggled on. "We have to talk about what you said at the funeral. You said you killed Jennie."

"Not so loud!" Don exclaimed hoarsely. "And not here."

He paused and looked up and down the hallway. He jerked his sleeves into place and pulled up the zipper before continuing, in more normal tones, "Look, can you come over to my house? We can talk there."

"Will your parents be home?"

"No."

Cathy thought for a moment. She knew her family rules: *Don't go to anyone's house if their parents aren't home, and don't go anywhere without letting someone know where you are.* Strict rules, but they made sense right now, with Jennie dead and the police maybe having the right killer and maybe not.

But she knew that she was going to break those rules this afternoon, if breaking them would help her find out what she needed to know. Then maybe poor Jennie's ghost would stop haunting her dreams at night.

"I'll be there," she said.

"Okay," said Don. He looked relieved, she thought—as if he, too, had made an important decision. "I'll meet you there."

Cathy went back to her own locker. Now that she'd committed herself to a meeting with Don, she was already starting to have second thoughts. *Suppose something goes wrong? Jennie's dead, and Don said he did it. You idiot, you could end up vanishing without a trace!*

Well, she could at least do something to prevent that. Cathy scribbled a quick message in her civics notebook: *Monday, October 17th. Gone to Don Fulman's house after school.* She tore out the sheet, folded it into a square, and put it in her locker on top of the neat stack of the books she didn't need.

There, that should do it. If anything happened to her, the school would clean out her locker, just as they had for Jennie. Someone would find the note, and Detective Rogers would have his suspect.

Cathy slammed the locker shut and turned her key in the padlock. Then she headed off on foot for Don's house in Gaspee Farms.

To her surprise, Don hadn't yet arrived when she showed up at the tidy, ranch-style house—almost identical to Jennie's, except for the color of the siding and the different flowers planted in the beds around the front. She rang the doorbell, and when no one answered she sat down on the doorstep to wait.

She felt conspicuous sitting there, and more than a little uneasy. The last time she'd come to Gaspee

Farms, she'd wound up talking to Detective Rogers down at the police station.

Rogers had thought someone was searching the Brodies' house for something. Something of Jennifer's—letters, maybe, or a diary.

Cathy smiled in spite of herself. If that was the case, the thief was out of luck. She knew that Jennie had thought keeping a diary was silly—the sort of thing you outgrew in junior high. And she hadn't needed to write letters, when all her friends were right here in Cresswell, and she could talk with them any time she wanted to.

Any time she wanted to.

Suddenly, Cathy stiffened. Jennie *had* been trying to talk to her, that night at Eric's party. She'd said so, before Don came up and took her off into the other room to dance. But Cathy had left before Jennie came back. She had gotten a ride home with Cheryl so she could get her clothes ready for that weekend in Fall River.

If I'd stayed a few minutes longer, would I have found out what Jennie wanted to tell me? And if I'd found out, would she still be alive today?

Then a blue sports car pulled up to the curb, and Don Fulman stepped out. He waved to the driver, and the car pulled away. Don walked up to the front steps.

"Hi, Cathy," he said.

Cathy got to her feet. "Was that Todd Barber?" she asked.

Don frowned. "Honestly, you and my mother.

Sure, it was Todd. Sometimes he gives me a ride home, you know? He had a couple of things to do on the way, so we ran a little late. Now, you said you wanted to talk about something."

Cathy drew a deep breath. "Yes."

"Okay, let's talk." Don pulled out a house key and let himself in. Then he gestured to Cathy to follow him. They walked into the living room, carpeted and furnished in heavy Mediterranean-style furniture. Don flung himself down into one of the big leather armchairs. Cathy sat down on the couch opposite and waited for Don to begin.

When he spoke, it wasn't quite what she'd expected. "You didn't tell anyone you were coming?"

Cathy thought about the note lying on top of her schoolbooks. That wasn't telling, not if she threw it out tomorrow morning.

"No," she said. "What's so important about not telling?"

"Telling things can get you killed."

"Are you talking about Jennie?"

Don nodded. "That's right."

"But she didn't tell anyone anything," Cathy protested. "If she *had* told someone, it would have been me."

"That's why you're in big trouble with certain people," Don said. "If they thought you knew . . ."

"I *don't* know," Cathy said. "If I did, I'd have told the police by now. And I haven't." She paused. "But somebody who does know probably should."

Don stood up again and began pacing nervously.

"Do you want some beer?" he asked. "My dad lets me drink it at home."

"No, thanks," she said. She could tell that Don was trying to change the subject. Whatever he had to say, he was fighting with himself to let it out, and she didn't want to stop him.

"Well, I'm going to have some," said Don, and he walked from the room, heading for what Cathy presumed was the kitchen.

Seconds later, a heavy thud seemed to hit Cathy's body like a blow, stunning her. All the lights went out. In the silence that followed came the brittle tinkling noise of falling glass, and a stream of thin acrid gray smoke drifted in from the direction of the kitchen.

Numbly, Cathy pulled herself to her feet. She forced herself to walk toward the kitchen and look through the open door.

The explosion had shattered all the windows and covered everything in the kitchen with a layer of soot. Beams of late-afternoon sunlight shone down through the smoke, illuminating what used to be the refrigerator—peeled open into strips of metal by the force of the blast.

Don Fulman lay in front of the smoking wreck. His face was a blackened ruin, its nose and lips gone, and empty sockets gaped where his eyes should have been. His hands had snapped off at the wrists. And nothing connected his shoulders and his hips but the few scraps of flesh still clinging to his bony spine.

Chapter 9

Cathy tried to scream, but the sound caught in her throat. Nothing came out but a strangled, choking noise. She turned from the blackened thing on the kitchen floor and ran—out of the house, away from the neighborhood, scarcely seeing or caring where her pounding footsteps took her.

She was several blocks away from the Fulmans' house when a city transit bus slowed to a halt at the corner ahead. The front and middle doors of the bus wheezed open, and people started climbing out— respectable people who wouldn't hesitate to call the police the instant they noticed that the door of the Fulmans' house was standing wide open during working hours on a weekday afternoon. Then Detective Rogers would come, if the neighbors hadn't summoned him as soon as they heard the explosion, and he'd find what was left of Don Fulman lying on the kitchen floor.

I've got to get out of here—it was less a coherent thought than a blind impulse to separate herself completely from what she had just seen. She didn't bother to check the destination or the route number but scrambled aboard the bus as soon as the last passenger had stepped off. She'd grabbed her purse and her books during her headlong dash through the Fulmans' living room—she didn't remember picking them up, but she had them with her now and was able to find a bus token to pay the fare.

Taking a window seat in the far back, she sat leaning her head against the cool glass. There was a wetness on her cheeks that left smear marks across the window; she looked at the smudged pane, then touched her face with one finger and realized that she had been crying.

Poor Don. He was about to tell me . . . about to tell me what? Who really killed Jennie? But if he knew that, why didn't he go to the police himself? Was it because he was afraid?

He'd had reason to be afraid. And now so did she.

The bus slowed to a stop at another corner, one that Cathy knew. Cresswell High School was only a few blocks away. She remembered the note she'd left in her locker, deliberately placed in plain view where the first person to open the door could see it—the note that named Don Fulman as a suspect if she never came back from Gaspee Farms. But now it was Don who was never coming back, and the only person the note would betray was Cathy Atmore—Cathy, whom the cops had questioned twice already and whom somebody had already tried to threaten into silence.

I have to get that note back before anybody finds it.

86

She got off the bus and headed for the high school, walking fast with her head down so that nobody would see her face and remember it later.

The school building was still open when she got there. Cathy slipped in unnoticed through one of the unlocked doors and made her way through the darkened halls of the main building to her locker. She pulled her key out, unlocked the padlock, and swung open the door.

The note was gone.

Frantically, she searched through all her textbooks, notebooks, and folders, with no result. The slip of white paper had vanished. *Maybe I never left it. Maybe I only imagined putting it on top of my civics book, because I was nervous and wanted to feel safe.*

She looked inside the notebook from which she'd torn the sheet of paper. The heavy pressure-marks of her ball-point pen still showed on the next page— she could make out the curve of a capital D and the two horizontal strokes of an F, close together on the same line. She'd written the note, all right. But someone else had broken into her locker and taken the note away, just as someone had broken into her locker the week before to leave the mutilated doll.

Cathy fought back a surge of blind terror. Whoever it was had known that she was going to be at Don's house. The doll had only been a warning. Had the bomb been meant for her? Whoever had set it would have had plenty of time, especially if they drove over to set the bomb while she walked and waited for bus connections. Or was it Don they were after, and they just didn't care if somebody else died at the same time?

She pushed the locker closed and turned away. She had to get home soon, before the Cresswell Transit Corporation buses went off their afternoon rush-hour schedule and came by the bus stop only once every hour or so. *I don't want to wait out there alone. Not tonight.*

Moving quickly, almost running, she headed back toward the front door. Then, in the lobby, she saw a figure, dimly silhouetted against the glass of the door. Dizzy with sudden fear, she nearly bolted and ran in the opposite direction before the waiting stranger said, "Cathy?"

It was Stu Martin's voice. He sounded startled. Cathy, for her part, came close to collapsing with relief.

"Stu," she said. "I never expected to see you here. I was afraid you were someone else."

"I—I never expected to see *you* here, either," Stu said.

Then the most surprising thing happened. Stu began to laugh, a high, whinnying sound through his nose, like a nervous horse. Cathy had never heard him laugh before—and now it seemed as if he would never stop.

The fear rose up in her again; she pushed past the weirdly giggling Stu and out the front door. A bus was approaching the stop outside the high school as she emerged onto the front steps. Cathy ran. She caught the bus just as the doors were closing.

Looking back, she saw that Stu Martin had come through the door after her. He was standing on the broad front steps of Cresswell High, watching the bus as it pulled away.

Cathy reached home just as her mother was setting the table for dinner. She expected to get a lecture for her lateness, but her mother only said, "That nice boy Todd Barber called. He told me you'd be a little late."

Cathy nodded without saying anything. Todd must have seen her sitting on the Fulmans' front steps when he dropped off Don. He couldn't have told her mom that, though, or Mrs. Atmore wouldn't be smiling. But why on earth had he bothered to call her mother?

In the living room, Cathy's father was watching the evening news. Cathy wandered in just as the screen changed from an antacid commercial to a picture of the Fulman home.

"Tragedy struck Cresswell High again today," the announcer intoned, "as the second student in a week died under mysterious circumstances. One week ago today, cheerleader Jennifer Brodie was found murdered in Johnson's Swamp. This afternoon, star halfback Donald Fulman died at his home in a freak explosion."

All the front windows of the Fulman house were broken out. *Funny, I never noticed the broken glass in the living room—just in the kitchen.* A collection of emergency vehicles filled the street and the driveway.

The ambulance hadn't left yet. Cathy thought about the broken, bloody thing she'd left on the kitchen floor, and she swallowed hard to keep her gorge from rising. No one would hurry Don to the hospital; he was beyond any doctor's help.

"Authorities refused to speculate on the cause of the explosion," the announcer continued, "although Northeast Gas employees spent over an hour checking the site."

Then a familiar figure appeared onscreen, coming out the door of the Fulmans' house—Detective Rogers. The police hadn't wasted any time in making the connection. First Jennie, then Don. And pretty soon, Cathy.

Cathy didn't get much sleep that night—she was too afraid of what her dreams might show her. The next day she forced herself to crawl out of bed and get dressed, although her arms and legs felt curiously inert, like bags of sand.

Yesterday's fear and today's exhaustion combined to leave her mind a fuzzy blur throughout most of her morning classes, and the fog didn't begin to lift until noon. Cathy was in the cafeteria sitting at her usual table. With both Jennie and Don gone, she felt even more out of place. She picked listlessly at her bowl of salad and listened to Todd and Pam and the others. She found their cheerful back-and-forth chatter oddly disturbing, coming as it did from people who'd just lost the second member of their crowd in the space of a week.

Something bad is going on. I can't put my finger on it, but I can tell that it's there.

A burst of nervous laughter a few tables away caught her attention. Cathy glanced in that direction and saw that Henry O'Toole was at it again. Holding up a fork loaded with what the menu board referred to as the Hot Entree, Henry proclaimed, "It never fails. Every time someone dies around here, they serve Breaded Veal Cutlet." He glanced over at the serving line, and lowered his voice conspiratorially. "Kind of makes you wonder what's in the Mystery Meat."

"Eww—*gross!*" exclaimed one girl at his table. Somebody else giggled.

"Did you see that Don was on the television last night?" asked Henry. He paused for effect. "And on the ceiling, and on the drapes, and on the *stove.* . . . Know why ol' Don's not going to ask a girl to go to the prom with him this year?"

"No, why?" said another student. Cathy, continuing to listen in spite of herself, thought it might be the one who had giggled.

Henry smirked. "No guts."

Cathy set her fork down next to her uneaten food and picked up her tray. "I can't take any more sick jokes," she said to no one in particular, and left the table. As she carried her tray over to the dirty-dish line, she saw Todd Barber and Matt Wilcox glance at each other and pick up their own trays. *What's up with them?*

They caught up with her just as her tray disappeared into the kitchen depths. "Hey, Cath," said Todd. "The gang's going out cruising this afternoon after school. Are you coming along?"

Cathy looked at them. The disoriented feeling she'd experienced during lunch was back again full force. She couldn't believe that they meant to go joy-riding—not twenty-four hours after losing Don, and only a week after losing Jennie. But Todd was standing there, his eyes almost unnaturally bright and cheerful, expecting an answer.

What would Jennie do right now? What does she want me to do?

"Sure," Cathy said aloud. "I'll come."

After school Cathy was waiting in the parking lot when Eric, Matt, Pam, and Stacy showed up together. They all piled together into Matt's BMW— Matt behind the wheel with Eric in the front seat beside him, and the two girls in the back seat with Cathy between them. Cathy had the distinct impression that the arrangement was deliberate.

I can't get out now. In more ways than one.

Matt fired up the engine. "Let's go!" he said. "Where to first?"

"How about the mall?" asked Stacy.

"Sounds good to me," agreed Eric.

"Fine," said Matt. The BMW headed out of the parking lot and purred down the street.

When they were out on the highway, Eric half-turned in the passenger seat to face the three girls. "You're probably wondering why we called you here," he said in a parody of the principal's most pompous school-assembly tones. Matt laughed, and on either side of Cathy, the two cheerleaders giggled.

Cathy tried to conceal her involuntary shiver. "Sort of," she admitted.

"It's like this," said Stacy. "We've decided that you're a good candidate for membership in the Booster Club."

"The Booster Club?" asked Cathy blankly. Cresswell High School had a lot of different student clubs —the Hackers' Club, the Drama Club, the Meteorology Club—but this was one she'd never heard of.

"It's the inner circle," said Pam. "You know, the kids who really run the school."

"The Booster Boss says we need to do some recruiting," said Eric from the front. "Membership has been down a bit lately."

Matt snickered. "*Way* down."

"Anyway," said Pam, "being a Booster is about the greatest thing there is. We're all members, and if you join, it puts you way ahead of everyone else."

Cathy wasn't quite sure what was going on. Did the others think she was dumb enough to take their offer at face value? Or did they care how she took it, as long as she went along with the game? *All right, if that's what you want . . .*

"What would I have to do?" she asked aloud. "Is this promoting the high school or something?"

Eric gave a brief snort of laughter. "You could say that," he replied.

"Careful," said Matt. "Don't spill any Booster Secrets before she joins."

"That's right," said Stacy. "You have to swear secrecy if you join," she explained to Cathy. "It's like a sorority or something, in college. No one ever tells the Booster Secrets."

"I see," said Cathy. She wondered if Pam knew how much she really *did* see, including a flash of memory from the day before—Don Fulman, sprawling in the leather armchair in his living room and saying, *"Telling things gets you killed."*

"You'll love the Booster Club," Pam assured Cathy. "You never have to worry about having a date for Friday night, or getting high grades, or missing school, or—oh, anything."

Cathy wetted her lips. "Okay. I'm in."

"You won't regret it," Stacy said. "We'll tell you the secret stuff after you're initiated and everything. But that comes later."

As she was speaking, the sign for the Pleasant Lane Mall appeared up ahead on the right. Matt took the exit and followed the service road beside the highway into the mall's parking area. He parked the BMW near the main entrance.

"Here we are," he said. "Let's go get some food, and after that you girls can do some shopping."

They went into the mall. First they had a quick snack at the Lucky Chicken stand in the Food Court, where Eric insisted on paying for everyone—"the Boosters have Booster Bucks" was how he put it. Then Pam and Stacy took Cathy away on a tour of the expensive little stores that filled the mall between the J. C. Penney's at one end and the Sears at the other. They finished up at the Silk 'n' Things boutique, a tiny shop with expensive decor and merchandise to match.

"This is my favorite place," said Pam. "I especially love their scarves. Look at this one—real silk." She pulled a red and blue scarf off the rack and held it out to Cathy. "Do you like it?"

"I suppose so," Cathy said after a long pause.

"Fine," said Pam. She turned to the shop attendant. "I'll take this one, please."

Cathy watched as Pam paid for the silk scarf with cash—"more Booster Bucks," the cheerleader explained while the clerk rang up the sale.

Outside the store, Pam took the scarf out of its paper bag and gave it to Cathy. "Here you go," she said, pressing the flimsy bit of cloth into Cathy's hand. "Now it's all official but the initiation. You're the latest member of the Booster Club."

Cathy looked silently at the expensive gift. She could have bought an entire dress for the price of that one little silk scarf, but that wasn't what had stopped the words in her mouth. What struck her mute was the realization that she'd seen red-and-blue-silk scarves exactly like this one, not long ago. Pam and Stacy both had them, and Jennie had worn one, just last week.

The day before she died.

Chapter 10

Cathy was mostly silent during the ride back to her family's house in the Upper Basin. The red-and-blue-silk scarf she'd put on at Pam's insistence seemed to curl around her throat like a noose. On the sidewalk, after Matt's BMW had disappeared from view, Cathy pulled off the scarf and stuffed it into her pocket. No use having her mother see it and ask where she'd gotten a thing like that.

Inside, she yelled hello to her mom and went straight upstairs to her room. Sitting at her desk, she took out a sheet of paper and wrote down everything she knew about what was going on. When Cathy had finished the list, she had two indisputable facts —Jennie and Don were both dead—and a whole page full of suspicions, most of them contradicting each other.

"*Something's going on with the school computer system,*" one sentence read. She followed that with Bill Madsen's name and a question mark, then, "*Who broke into my locker yesterday afternoon?*"

"*Something funny is going on with the guys in the Booster Club,*" another sentence read. "*I think they* know something about Jennie and Don." Then on the next line, "*Jennie wanted to tell me something, and so did Don. Now Jennie and Don are dead.*"

Another blank line, then, "*Stu Martin's been acting weird lately. Does he know something, too? Do they all know something? AM I THE ONLY PERSON AT CRESSWELL HIGH SCHOOL WHO DOESN'T KNOW WHAT'S GOING ON?*"

Cathy sat for a long time looking at the list, with the last question scrawled across the bottom in angry, slashing letters. Then she tore up the paper, flushed the pieces down the toilet, and went downstairs to dinner.

Next morning at school, Cathy took the Booster scarf out of her coat pocket and knotted it around her throat, the way Jennie had worn hers at Eric's party. Maybe wearing the scarf would bring her—well, not luck exactly, but some kind of closeness to what Jennie had been trying to tell her that night.

Results came sooner than Cathy expected. She was about to close her locker door and head for homeroom when Stacy came up to her. The cheerleader had a smile on her face and a red-and-blue-silk scarf peeking out of the collar of her blouse.

"You don't really need all those books," she said to Cathy. "Come on, let's cut class today."

"I don't know," Cathy said. "I skipped last week, and you wouldn't believe the trouble I got into. Mr. Lipton told my parents I might get suspended if I did it again."

"You won't get into any trouble," Stacy assured her. "Trust me, the Boosters do this all the time."

Cathy fingered the silk scarf at her neck. *The Booster Club is part of everything that's going on. I owe it to Jennie.*

"Well, okay," she said aloud, "if you say nothing will happen."

"Don't worry," said Stacy. "No one will ever know—the club's got a really great system going. Come on, Booster Girl!"

Stacy and Cathy walked out of the building and down to the parking lot. "We'll take Matt's car," Stacy said, pulling out a set of keys from her purse. "As long as I get it back before school's out, everything will be fine."

Stacy led the way to the BMW and slid into the driver's seat. "I won't have to do this much longer," the cheerleader said as Cathy got into the front seat beside her. "Before long I'll have enough Booster Bucks to get a car of my own."

"You can get that many Booster Bucks?" Cathy asked. Her mouth felt dry. *If she tells me the Boosters are selling magazine subscriptions, I'm not going to believe her.*

But Stacy offered no explanation. "Sure you can," she said. "How do you think Don Fulman was planning to get *his* car?"

Cathy glanced at Stacy. The cheerleader had pronounced Don's name without a tremor—she certainly didn't sound like someone who'd just had a close friend die a gruesome death. Don had been a longtime member of Stacy's crowd.

And he knew what was going on. He was about to tell me, and he died. Just like Jennie. But I haven't told anyone yet, so they think they can buy me off instead.

Cathy swallowed hard and said aloud, "Right. You can have a lot of fun in Cresswell if you've got wheels and cash and your time is your own."

"That's the Booster spirit!" said Stacy approvingly. "What do you say we have brunch in Lapham Corners? There's a quaint little bistro over there—the Green Umbrella. I'll explain everything then."

Cathy could only nod. Lapham Corners was a small town—a village, really, far out in the undeveloped countryside beyond the houses of Rocky Banks Estates. The people who lived there were so well off, they were almost invisible. Brunch at the Green Umbrella would probably cost enough to pay the Atmores' grocery bill for a month.

More Booster Bucks. Cathy felt a sudden surge of anger. *These people think that an expensive scarf and some fancy food can make me forget about Jennie. Well, they're wrong!*

Not long after that, Cathy sat looking at Stacy across a linen tablecloth set with crystal and silver. The waiter had just brought them the brunch Stacy had ordered—shrimp quiche with almonds, fresh asparagus, and tiny potatoes steamed in their jackets. Stacy thanked the waiter by name.

"Save room for dessert," the cheerleader advised

Cathy after the waiter had left. "They bring around a truly outstanding pastry cart."

"It's a long way from Chopped Beef Patty with Brown Gravy," Cathy conceded. "But how does all this work? Why doesn't the school call our parents and tell them we're not in class?"

"It's easy," said Stacy. "You know the big computer that keeps track of attendance and grades and everything?"

Cathy nodded.

"Well, it makes the calls, too. But not for us. It's part of being in the Booster Club—none of your absences ever show up on the main system. And you don't have to worry about grades, either, because the computer writes the report cards, and the Boosters own the computer." Stacy leaned forward and lowered her voice. "We can do *anything*."

"You're not kidding," said Cathy. She took a sip of her ice water to cover her dismay. What Stacy had described was the work of an expert with computers, and none of the Boosters she'd met so far came even close.

Somebody else is doing all their hacking for them, Cathy realized. *The Boosters may think they own the system, but they don't. Somebody else is buying them off with free class cuts and faked report cards and all those Booster Bucks, the same way they're trying to buy me. And it works, too. Whoever runs the system runs the Boosters.*

Cutting class, Cathy eventually decided, wasn't nearly as much fun as it was cracked up to be. She wasn't particularly fond of driving aimlessly around town, even in a BMW, and she'd seen all the shops in the mall yesterday afternoon. When the time came for Stacy to return Matt's car to the school lot, Cathy felt secretly relieved. She'd call Cheryl as soon as she got home, she told herself, and get all the class assignments. The school office might not know she'd been absent, but Osgood the Grouch certainly would.

She was upstairs in her room working her way through the English assignment—another chapter of *Silas Marner*, which Cathy privately considered to be the dullest book in the English language—when the telephone rang.

"Cathy, it's for you!" called her mother from downstairs.

Cathy hurried down to the phone.

"Hi, Cathy," said Todd Barber. "How was your first day as a Booster?"

"Just great," Cathy lied. "I had a wonderful time."

"That's good," said Todd. "I told the Booster Buddy you'd fit right in. Listen, the club's getting together after school tomorrow. Will you be there?"

"I think so," Cathy said. She wondered if this time she'd get to learn some more of the Booster Secrets—like the source of all those free-flowing Booster Bucks. "I have to ask my mom, though."

She covered the receiver with one hand and called, "Mom, can I go out tomorrow afternoon?"

"Who with?" her mother inquired from the kitchen. "And where?"

"Todd Barber, and—" Cathy spoke into the receiver again. "Where will we be going?"

"Just to the mall," Todd reassured her. "No big deal. We'll be back before five."

Cathy relayed the information to her mother.

"As long as you're with friends," Mrs. Atmore said, "I suppose it's all right. But don't go near any strangers, and don't stay out after dark."

"I won't, Mom," Cathy promised. To Todd, she said, "It's okay. I'll see you after school." She paused. "That reminds me—I need the homework assignment for math class. Have you got it?"

Todd laughed. "Are you kidding? I had better things to do. Look, Cath, gotta run. See you tomorrow."

He hung up. Cathy went back to her desk and did all the math problems at the end of the next section, just to make sure of having done the ones that had been assigned. While she worked, she frowned over the thought that remained in the back of her head: Something was going on at Cresswell besides a hacker playing games with the computer system. Fake grades and rigged attendance sheets might be fun for the Boosters, but they didn't provide the kind of money the Boosters had been throwing around, and they weren't enough to kill for.

The next day passed quickly. Once again she wore the red-and-blue Booster scarf, as an invitation to

102

she wasn't certain what. Trouble possibly, but if so, it was slow in coming. In spite of yesterday's absence, she was overprepared for her math class; and in first-period history Mr. Osgood only looked at her above his glasses without comment as she handed in two days' homework at once.

Nothing exceptional happened all day, in fact, except for a brief incident in the hallway after third period, just before lunch. A student she didn't know, a sophomore, came up to her as she was stashing her books into her locker.

"Do you have any stuff for me?" he asked.

"What do you mean, 'stuff'?" Cathy asked, puzzled.

"Come on," he said. "Don't play games. I need it bad—I have a test coming up. I gotta study."

Cathy shook her head. "I'm sorry. I don't know what you're talking about."

The kid was getting angry now. "You've got *that,*" he said, pointing at her red-and-blue scarf. "So don't play games with me. I pay enough, don't I?"

"I think you have me confused with somebody else," Cathy said firmly.

She turned away quickly before the boy could answer. *I don't like the sound of this,* she thought as she hurried toward the cafeteria. *What did he think I was selling?*

During lunch at the crowd's usual table, she mentioned the incident, although without bringing up any of her suspicions. Stacy frowned.

"Not so loud," she said. "What did the guy look like?"

Cathy told her.

"Okay, I know who that is," said Stacy. "I'll take care of it." Then the cheerleader frowned at Todd Barber. "You didn't tell her last night?"

"The Booster Buddy said to wait until after the initiation," Todd said. "I was going to lay it all out for her this afternoon after school." He turned to Cathy. "We're still on, right?"

Cathy nodded. "Right."

The school day dragged on. Cathy had a hard time concentrating during her classes. She took notes automatically, her mind scarcely comprehending what her hand was writing, and she promised herself that she'd read over the pages later, when she wasn't so nervous.

If there is a later, she caught herself thinking as she retrieved her coat from her locker after last period. If knowing the Booster Secrets had killed first Jennie and then Don, then once Cathy knew the secrets, she too would be walking on the edge of a cliff.

As long as they think they've bought me, I'm safe. But the instant they realize the truth, I'll be as dead as Jennie.

Oddly enough, instead of frightening Cathy, thinking of Jennie only strengthened her resolve. She went on down to the parking lot where the other Boosters were waiting.

This time they took two cars, Todd's and Matt's. Cathy didn't protest when she wound up riding alone with Todd, although the isolation made her nervous. But then, instead of heading for the mall, Todd turned in the other direction and started driving through the Upper Basin toward the Lower Basin.

"I thought you said we were going to the mall," Cathy said.

"New plans," said Todd smoothly. "It's initiation time, so we're headed for the Booster Clubhouse instead."

Cathy blinked. "Oh," she said. "That's okay, then."

She spent the next few minutes concentrating on not looking as frightened as she felt. Todd drove into the heart of the Lower Basin, where old warehouses and abandoned industrial buildings lined the river. Her uneasiness grew as Todd turned off the main road and down a series of alleys between high brick walls. Finally he pulled up outside a low building of sooty brick. The doors were chained shut and padlocked. Matt's BMW was parked nearby.

Cathy wet her lips. "Where are we?" she asked.

"The Booster Clubhouse, like I told you," Todd said. "It's an old deserted mill. Nobody ever comes here."

"It sounds perfect," Cathy managed to say. *In more ways than one*, added a frightened voice in her head. Johnson's Swamp was out in this direction; if she'd misjudged the Boosters' intentions, her "initiation" might be a one-way trip into its brackish waters. Oh, yes, the factory made a perfect place for secret meetings—and a perfect place for taking someone who would never return alive.

But the other Boosters were climbing out of Matt's BMW, and Matt was unlocking the padlock on the doors of the mill.

Todd opened the door on his side of the car. "Come on," he said. "It's initiation time."

I can't back out now. Jennie would never forgive me. She glanced around her. *The Boosters wouldn't forgive me, either.*

She climbed out of the car and joined the others at the door of the mill. "I'm ready," she said.

Stacy produced a strip of black cloth. "We're going to have to blindfold you for the ceremony," she said. "It's part of the rules."

Cathy made no protest as Pam and Stacy tied the black cloth around her eyes and led her forward into a large, echoing space—the courtyard of the old mill, she supposed, because she could still feel the sun's warmth on her head. Someone pressed a round object into her hands; from the shape she guessed that it might be a human skull, though the slick surface under her fingers suggested that the Boosters used a plastic model rather than the real thing.

Todd Barber's voice came from close behind her. "Are you willing to take the oath and become a member of the Booster Club?"

"I am," said Cathy.

"Then repeat after me: 'I, Cathy Atmore . . .'"

"I, Cathy Atmore . . ." she repeated, her voice bouncing back at her eerily from unseen walls.

106

" 'Do solemnly swear . . .' "

"Do solemnly swear . . ."

" 'That I will never reveal the secrets of the Booster Club . . .' "

"That I will never reveal the secrets of the Booster Club," echoed Cathy.

" 'And will follow without question the orders of the Booster Boss . . .' "

"And will follow without question the orders of the Booster Boss . . ."

" 'Or hope to die.' "

Oh, Jennie. Is that what you promised, too?

Cathy drew a deep breath and hoped her voice would be steady for the final words of the Booster Oath.

"Or hope to die."

Chapter 11

Cathy felt somebody's hands working at the knot of the blindfold. The strip of black cloth fell away from her eyes, and she could see again. She looked down at the object in her hands, and saw that she'd guessed right—it was, in fact, a skull, one of the cheap plastic ones you could buy in joke shops and novelty stores.

The other members of the Booster Club gathered around her. Todd Barber reclaimed the plastic skull, saying, "Congratulations! Now you're a full-fledged Booster. For life."

"What do you mean, 'for life'?" Cathy asked.

"That's one of the Booster Secrets," Stacy told her. "You can't go back once you're in. If you do, the Booster Boss will know."

"Yeah," said Matt Wilcox. "And remember, you promised 'hope to die.' Just like Don."

"Jennie hoped to die, too," put in Eric. His eyes were bright, as Todd's had been at lunch the other day, and his pupils were dilated. The other Boosters laughed.

He's on something. They're all on something. Cathy

blinked at them through her thick glasses and hoped that she looked as dense as they obviously thought she was. "Uh . . . got it," she said after a long pause. "But which of you is the Booster Boss?"

The Boosters looked uneasy for a moment. Then Todd Barber moved in, smooth as always, to cover the awkward silence. "He isn't here. The Boss passes along his orders through the Booster Buddy."

"The Booster Buddy? Who's he?" asked Cathy.

She would have bet a month's lunch money that none of the Boosters had ever seen their mysterious Boss at all. She wondered if he even existed. Could the Booster Buddy—whoever that was—have invented the Boss, just for dramatic effect? Or maybe the Boss was real, but not a Cresswell High student at all? A teacher, maybe, or somebody in town?

"I'll introduce you to the Booster Buddy at school tomorrow," promised Pam. "In the meantime, just remember: Good Boosters don't ask questions."

The rest of the meeting was an anticlimax as far as Cathy was concerned. She still didn't know where the Boosters got their money—from something illegal, that was clear, but nobody seemed willing to tell her what. *They don't really trust me. But if I'm lucky, they think they've either bought me off with the Booster Bucks or scared me off with the Booster Oath. If I'm not lucky . . .*

She put the thought out of her mind and concentrated on keeping up with Pam and Stacy's flow of light chatter. She still had trouble believing that the deaths of Jennie and Don were affecting them so little. Even if the Boosters were the ones responsible, she would have expected them to feel *something* about the whole situation. But you couldn't have told from their talk that Don and Jennie had been anything more than distant acquaintances who'd met with some kind of unfortunate accident.

Poor Jennie. Why did you ever join them, anyhow? Was it just to make Don happy? How long did you know their secrets before this Boss of theirs decided that you had to die?

Now that the initiation was over, the meeting at the old mill showed signs of turning into a prolonged party. Matt had a cooler in his car, filled with ice cubes and assorted drinks in cans—Coke and Pepsi on top, and beer underneath. Cathy didn't know what else the back of the BMW might contain, and she didn't really want to ask.

She turned to Todd Barber. "I hate to sound like a nerd or something," she said, "but I promised my mom I'd be back home before dark. And when Mom gets nervous, she starts telephoning everyone in the world. Real embarrassing."

As she'd hoped, Todd looked at her askance for a moment, then muttered, "You're not kidding," and headed for his car. "C'mon, then—I can drop you off."

Cathy arrived at her house just as the long shadows of late afternoon began to deepen into twilight. Inside the house, the smell of roast beef filled the air.

"You promised me that you'd be home before dark, Cathy," said Mrs. Atmore from the kitchen.

Her mother didn't sound too upset, though; Cathy supposed twilight wasn't dark enough to count as long as she hadn't missed supper, too.

"It's still light out," said Cathy. "Do you need me to set the table?"

She was already getting dishes and silverware out of the old walnut sideboard as she spoke. The meal tonight would be a good one, because her father was leaving in the morning for another long haul down I-95. As usual on a night when Mr. Atmore was about to go on the road, the table conversation consisted of a lot of back-and-forth worrying: Mrs. Atmore fretting about bad weather, bad roads, and bad drivers who might complicate her husband's trip, and Mr. Atmore cautioning his wife and daughter about prowlers, burglars, and young men with bad intentions.

"I especially don't like the idea of you and Cath being unprotected at a time like this," Mr. Atmore concluded during dessert. "You both know where I keep the shotgun—and before I leave on this run, it'll be loaded. So if anybody shows up looking like trouble, you get it out right then."

On the other side of town, in Rocky Bank Estates, Bill Madsen sat in his darkened bedroom, watching the glowing green letters that scrolled up the computer monitor in front of him. He'd spent the better part of the past five days working with his home computer system. He'd always devoted most of his spare time and extra cash to the care and feeding of the silicon beast, and at the moment time was what he had plenty of.

He hadn't been back to Cresswell High since he had been released under his parents' recognizance. He wasn't suspended, since technically he wasn't guilty of anything until after he'd had a proper trial. But the principal and the vice-principal had made it clear, politely, to his parents, that while the Doctors William and Elizabeth Madsen might have enough money to hire the very best lawyers, it might be best for all concerned if Bill didn't return to Cresswell "until this distasteful episode is over."

Right now, while Bill was stuck at home awaiting arraignment, he took a great deal of comfort from the opinion of Felton Carruthers (of the Providence law firm Carruthers, Wharton, Dedham, and Nighe) that the Cresswell District Attorney didn't have a case—or not much of one, anyway. "It's circumstantial, that's all," Carruthers had said. "As long as the State can't put you in that swamp on that night with a knife in your hand, you'll get a directed verdict of not guilty."

Then Carruthers had looked straight at Bill. "They *don't* have a witness who can say you were there, do they?"

"No," Bill had replied. "They don't."

"In that case," Carruthers said, looking as relieved as a man who wears a twenty-four-hour poker face can, "the presumption of innocence is on our side. They'd be foolish to even let it come to trial. In the meantime, keep a low profile and don't talk to

112

anybody the prosecution might want to subpoena as a witness."

That had been a week ago. Now, with little else to occupy his time, Bill sat in the dark and watched the lines of type march across his screen. He had his own telephone line just for the computer system, and with it he could dial up and get access to computer networks and bulletin board systems all over the country—from the big commercial nets where hundreds of users came and went electronically every day, to small setups like the BBS at Cresswell High. You could see a lot that way, when you were as good with computers as he was; you could watch everywhere without touching anything, and without leaving a trace behind. He straightened and leaned forward as a particularly interesting message came up on the screen.

"Boss, this is Buddy," it read. *"Atmore is in, but Number One doesn't trust her. What should we do? Maybe you could check her out."*

Yes, that *was* an interesting message. He'd have to do something about it, too. He logged off-line and reached for the telephone. He had a call or two to make.

Upstairs in the Atmore house, Cathy worked at her English assignment—another interminable chapter of *Silas Marner*, not made any more interesting by the fact that compared with her, Silas didn't have any problems. When the phone rang and her mother called, "Cathy! It's for you!" she laid the novel aside with relief and ran down to the living room to pick up the extension.

"Hello?" she said.

"Cathy?" said a half-familiar voice on the other end. "This is Bill Madsen—from school, remember? The Hackers' Club?"

"I remember," said Cathy tightly. *You're the guy who the cops think killed my best friend. So what are you calling me for at eight o'clock on a school night?*

Bill hurried on. "I need to talk with you about something."

"Okay, talk."

"Not on the phone. Could you come over?"

"I . . . don't know. I'd have to ask my mom."

"Don't do that," Bill said quickly. "Don't tell anyone."

"Why not?"

"I'm not supposed to talk to anybody—but I need to talk with you. There's something going on at school. I think you're in danger."

Cathy looked over her shoulder. Nobody was within earshot. She lowered her voice. "I'll have to think about it. I'm still not sure I—" She heard her father's heavy footsteps coming from the direction of the kitchen, and she switched hastily to more ordinary tones. "No problem—I'm just glad I could help. I'll see you in class tomorrow. 'Bye."

She hung up the phone as her father came into the living room. "Some friend of yours stuck with his homework?" he asked.

"A class problem," she told him. "But we managed to work it out, I think."

She hurried upstairs before she had to bend the truth any further. Behind the closed door of her bedroom, she sat at her desk with *Silas Marner* lying open but unread in front of her.

What do I do? Why should I trust Bill when the cops all think he's guilty? She shook her head. *But is he really dumb enough to have hidden Jennie's legs in his own mom's car? Never mind what the police think—do I really in my heart think that Bill's the one who did it?*

And the answer, it appeared, was that she didn't. Someone from Cresswell High School had been involved in Jennie's death, that much seemed certain —but Cathy couldn't help feeling that she'd stood a lot closer to him this afternoon in the Booster Clubhouse than she ever had down in the computer lab.

But was a feeling like that enough to take a risk on? Maybe she ought to wait until daytime tomorrow to see Bill. She could take advantage of the Boosters' private arrangement and cut school for the afternoon. That would give her plenty of time to hear what Bill wanted to tell her, and she could still make it home before dark.

Wait—asked a voice in the back of her head. *Like Don Fulman did?* He'd waited a bit too long to talk, and now he was dead without talking at all. And what about Jennie? If Cathy had stuck with her that Friday night, she might have told her everything in time for someone to save her life. If Cathy waited this time, would another freak accident or insane killer silence Bill, too?

"No!" she said aloud. "This time I'm going to do it now."

Quickly, before her courage failed, she stood up and turned out the lamp on her desk. When her parents came upstairs, they wouldn't see any light coming out from under her door, and they would assume she'd fallen asleep. She put on a navy blue jacket and a matching knit cap—never mind the flat hair she'd have in the morning, she needed the dark garments to help her sneak out unnoticed—and retrieved her change purse with its supply of bus tokens from her shoulder bag. Then she went over to the window and pushed it open.

The cold autumn air blew in across the sill, making her shiver. It had been a long time since she'd gone out of her room this way, not since she was a kid and Jennie still lived next door. They'd played pirates and rescues during the summer, and this had been the secret way out of the tower prison—slipping out through the window onto the roof of the garage, then pussyfooting across the shingles to the maple tree in the side yard and sliding down the trunk to the ground. But now the games were over. Jennie was dead.

Jennie, I'm doing this for you.

Cathy looked back once into her darkened room, stepped across the windowsill onto the garage, and slid the window shut behind her.

Chapter 12

Cathy made her way unnoticed across the garage roof, down the maple tree, and out to the street. The night was dark and windy. High streamers of cloud blew across the face of the moon and then away again, lending the streets a patchy, intermittent light.

She kept to the shadows as best she could. Bill had said she was in danger. She didn't know what he'd found out—or even if she ought to believe him —but she knew she was playing a dangerous game. The Booster Club had killed Jennie Brodie, Cathy was sure of that. All it would take was for one member of the club to decide that Cathy hadn't really meant to keep her oath, and she would wind up as dead as Jennie.

She hurried through the pool of light coming out of the windows of the Late-Nite Laundromat. How would the Boosters try to silence her? Cathy wondered. If they had any sense, after two messy murders they really ought to go for something uncomplicated and ordinary-looking.

That's what I'd do. Something like a hit-and-run acci-

dent or a mugging, for example. She shivered. For the rest of the walk to the bus stop, she kept looking over her shoulder and jumped nervously every time an automobile drove past.

At the bus stop, she fished out a token from her change purse and kept it ready in her hand. She could ride on this route all the way past Four Corners to the far side of Gaspee Farms, and then walk from there to Bill's house on Alouette Lane in Rocky Banks. She'd have to be careful again for the last bit, she thought; the Madsens lived right next door to Eric Skidwell.

Cathy waited in the shadows near the corner, her back against the wall of the laundromat. She didn't know how long she would have to stand there; the buses didn't come as often at night. Minutes passed. She started at a noise in the shadows, then almost collapsed with relief when it turned out to be a stray dog looking through a trash can.

This is ridiculous. What am I doing out here, anyway? I could be walking right into the house of a real sicko— never mind just the ordinary trouble I could get into hanging around a bus stop at night.

She was at the point of turning around and going home when she saw an indistinct figure coming toward her along the sidewalk. As the figure moved from the shadows to the pools of light below the streetlamps, Cathy saw that it was a girl—a young girl with blond hair, just like Jennie's. She was walking with a strange, stiff-legged gait—as if, Cathy

thought, her legs had been cut off and sewn back on.
Even in the light, her face was still in shadow.

That's because she has *no face,* thought Cathy frantically as a familiar voice—Jennie's voice—whispered faintly, *Help me, Cath. Help me.*

Cathy could feel a scream trying to get past the sudden tightness in her throat. Then, blessedly, the bus pulled up to the corner, blocking out the nightmare. A wave of warm air rushed out as the doors sighed open. Cathy didn't hesitate. She stepped forward, ran up the steps of the bus without looking back, and took a seat up front near the driver.

The doors closed, and the bus moved forward past the place where the apparition had been. Cathy forced herself to look out the window. No faceless young girl stood on the sidewalk beneath the streetlight—only an old lady with white hair, a homeless woman moving stiffly along on her way to who-knew-where.

Cathy sank back against the cracked plastic seat and closed her eyes. *I'm starting to see things. If this doesn't end soon, they're going to wrap me up in a nice white jacket and haul me off to the funny farm.*

At least she was doing something now, not just waiting for the next dreadful thing to happen. Nothing else upset her journey—no waking nightmares on the bus, no strange car roaring at her out of the dark during the walk through Rocky Banks Estates. At last she stood on Alouette Lane outside the Madsens' house, a big, low building set well back from the road and shielded from view by trees. Eric's

119

house lay uphill around the curve of the lane, separated from the Madsens' by more trees and shrubbery.

"Don't do anything stupid," Detective Rogers had said. She couldn't get rid of the feeling that she was doing something *really* stupid, so rather than stand and think about it, she started walking toward Bill's house. She knew her way; she'd been to Eric's place more than once, and this block was familiar.

She drew closer to the house. Light shone out onto the lawn from a big window near the front, where white lace curtains gave a fuzzy view of bookcases and a sofa. A woman moved into the light—Bill's mother, Cathy supposed. Bill himself was nowhere in view.

Cathy moved away from the front windows and started circling around toward the back of the house. Maybe Bill's room was back there somewhere. She hoped he'd have a light on so she could find it. She didn't want to have to creep up and look into the windows of a bunch of darkened rooms one at a time. It was probably dangerous, not to mention illegal.

There was only one light burning at the back of the house. Cathy moved cautiously up to the window and looked inside. The room was a boy's bedroom, with a big stereo and a lot of computer equipment. Bill sat at the desk, reading a book and listening to something on earphones.

Cathy hesitated. This was it. Did she have the

nerve to knock on the window, or would she turn around and go home?

Am I doing the right thing, Jennie? Is this the best way to help you—or do the police have the right idea, and I'm heading for a heart-to-heart talk with the last person you ever saw in your life?

Telling herself not to be stupid, nothing could happen to her as long as Bill's mom was in the house, she reached up and knocked on the window. Bill didn't turn around—the earphones—so she knocked again, louder, and then a third time. By now the rapping of her knuckles against the glass sounded so loud, she thought the whole house would hear her.

Finally Bill looked up. His eyes slowly focused on the window. Then they widened behind his glasses as he realized there was someone standing outside. He took off the earphones, came over to the window, and opened it.

"Cathy?" he asked quietly. "I'd about decided you weren't going to show up."

"I had to take the bus," she said.

He leaned out the window and extended his hand. "Well, come on inside. We need to talk."

Half-reluctantly, Cathy allowed herself to be helped over the low window sill into Bill's room. He shut the window after her, then went over to the stereo system and unplugged the earphones. Music filled the room—something classical that Cathy didn't recognize.

"We can talk now," Bill said under the cover of

121

the music. He motioned her to the chair by the desk. Cathy sat down, and Bill seated himself on the floor across the room, his back against the sliding door of the closet.

"Okay," he said. "It's like this. I was . . . well, looking around the school's bulletin board system— I can do it from here, and frankly I don't have all that much else to occupy my time right now—and I found a really weird message. About you."

Cathy looked at Bill, trying to figure out if he was serious, or if this was just a bad joke on the way to something a whole lot worse. She couldn't see any malice in his expression, but that didn't mean much. Maybe he was one of those sick people who didn't feel anything no matter what awful things they did.

Or maybe he's just a shy guy in glasses without very many friends.

"What about me?" she asked aloud.

"Somebody's worried about you," Bill said. "What do you know about a couple of people who call themselves 'Boss' and 'Buddy'?"

"I don't know who they are," Cathy said quickly.

"Well, they know who you are. There's only one Atmore in Cresswell High, and you're it. In the message, Buddy was telling Boss that you were 'in,' but that someone else called Number One didn't trust you." He paused. "Want to tell me what it was you got into? There's been something funny going on with the computer system lately—I've been watching it—and I think these Boss and Buddy characters are part of the problem."

Cathy still hesitated. *You're this far,* said the voice in her head that had been urging her onward since she left the house. *Quit playing halfway games. Either trust him, or don't.*

"There's a club," she said, talking fast now, before she could lose her nerve. "They call themselves the Boosters. The big-time jocks are in it—Eric and Todd and Matt, and Don was, too—and a couple of the cheerleaders. I think Jennie joined them just before she died. She found out something, I don't know what exactly. So they killed her. Don, too, because he was about to crack and tell the secret after Jennie died. They don't know whether Don and Jennie told me anything or not—they've been trying to bring me into the group so they can control me, I think. There's money involved; all the Boosters have lots of it."

"What about Boss and Buddy?"

Cathy thought she heard a note of contempt in Bill's voice.

"Somebody called the Booster Boss runs the whole show," she said. "I get the impression nobody in the club has ever seen him—or it could be a her, for all I know. The Boosters only talk to somebody they call the Booster Buddy. I don't know who he is, either."

"Right," said Bill. "A secret club can't be the whole point, though. Most schools have one or two of those, and they all manage to get along without cutting people into pieces or blowing them up."

"I think they're selling something," Cathy said.

"Drugs, maybe." She told Bill about the kid who'd approached her in the hall that morning, when she was wearing her Booster scarf. "But I don't know what kind, or where they get them—maybe through this Boss of theirs."

"They can't be getting them from someone in town," Bill said. "The police probably have a pretty good idea who's selling what locally, and to whom. If whoever killed Jennie was tied into that network, the cops would have traced the connection by now and broken the whole case." He thought for a minute. "It must be something they're making themselves. Uppers, maybe—stimulants. They're dead simple to make if you've stayed awake in chemistry class. That's probably where Boss and Buddy come in," he added, again with that fleeting note of contempt. "Those jocks have the collective IQ of a set of bowling pins. Someone else has to be the brains of the operation."

"Stimulants," mused Cathy. "My dad says some truck drivers use them to keep awake on long hauls. And that kid said he had a test coming up."

"Right," said Bill. "Study all night and never need to sleep. Cheap at the price, if you don't mind scrambling your brains a little in the process."

Standing up, he went over to a bookshelf in the corner of the room and pulled out a reference manual of some sort. "Here we go," he said. " 'The abuser of stimulants may exhibit restlessness or nervousness, with tremors in the hands, dilated pupils, a dry mouth, and heavy perspiration. He is usually talkative, and he may have delusions and hallucinations if he has used a large quantity. Dangerous, aggressive behavior with antisocial effects is common among abusers of stimulants. In serious cases amphetamines, one type of stimulant, cause a psychosis which resembles schizophrenia.' "

Cathy looked at Bill as he closed the book and slid it back into place on the shelf. "That other kid at school," she said. "The one they had to take away, who thought he had bugs all over him—"

"Classic symptom," Bill said. "Absolutely classic. You'd better be careful around your Booster pals from now on. People who use amphetamines can be seriously crazy."

Cathy's mouth felt dry. "Crazy enough to kill people?"

"Big time," said Bill. "Remember that 'dangerous antisocial behavior'? I can't think of anything much more antisocial than murder."

"What about what happened to Don Fulman?" she asked. "Could they have done that? Wouldn't they have had to buy the explosives?"

"Not necessarily," Bill said. "Anyone who could make amphetamines could probably make explosives and rig a bomb, too. All you have to do is—"

"Stay awake in chemistry class. I know."

"—just unplug the refrigerator, attach the detonator to the light inside, close the door, and plug the refrigerator back in. Sooner or later, the guy you're after is going to want a Coke or something, and then —boom."

He didn't say anything else for a while but sat staring out into the middle distance while the music on the stereo played on. "So we have a theory," he said at last. "It still doesn't get us anywhere."

"We could tell the police."

Bill shook his head. "What good would that do? I'd just be trying to find someone else to take the rap for me—and what have you got, except for hearsay and speculation?"

Cathy shrugged. Another long silence followed. Then the glimmerings of an idea occurred to her. "Maybe if we got some proof—"

"How? I don't want to get too far into this. My lawyer told me to stay clear of anyone and anything connected with the case. He'd have fits if he knew I was talking to you right now."

"The Boosters skip school and then doctor the main attendance record," Cathy told him. "If I cut class tomorrow, maybe you could sort of hang around the computer files like you've been doing, and see who comes on-line to change my absent mark before the automatic dialing program cuts in."

"Okay, I can try that," said Bill. "But that won't do either of us much good if we can't tell Detective Rogers who the Boss and the Buddy are."

"I'm supposed to meet the Buddy sometime tomorrow," Cathy said.

"Great news," said Bill. "Go right home when you skip class, and wait for me to call. We have to be able to get in touch. Once we've got that bit of information, we can put a whole bunch more of the pieces together."

"Just like a puzzle, right?" said Cathy, a bit bitterly. *Jennie's dead, and he's treating this like some kind of game.*

She stood up. "I've got to go. Buses only run once an hour this time of night, and I don't want to miss the next one."

"Fine," said Bill. He stood up, too, and slid open the window. "Maybe this will work. In any case it'll give Rogers someone to think about besides us. But listen, please don't tell anyone about this until we have a chance to talk again. We need something good before we can go to the police with it, and anyone could be the Buddy and the Boss. You don't know who to trust."

Cathy climbed out over the sill, and Bill slid the window shut behind her, leaving her alone in the dark of the cold lawn.

Cathy glanced back in through the window. Bill was listening to his headphones again, reading his book, as if no one had disturbed him.

"Great," Cathy muttered under her breath. "Someone else telling me not to talk with anyone. Just what I need." She cut across the lawn to the sidewalk, then down to the bus stop and back home. The whole way home she wondered if she had done the right thing, or if she had just gotten herself deeper in trouble.

Chapter 13

Cathy made it back to the Upper Basin without any problems, in spite of her misgivings. Climbing up the maple tree to the garage roof wasn't any harder now than it had been when she was a kid, though she hadn't gone this way in years and this was the first time she'd tried it in the dark. Her parents never knew that she'd been gone. She undressed and tumbled into bed, to awaken what felt like only minutes later with the sunlight in her eyes. She hadn't dreamed at all.

Jennie didn't talk to me last night. Maybe that means I'm on the right track, she thought later that morning as she hung her coat up in her locker. The next step, she knew, was to get herself introduced to the Booster Buddy, then skip out of school so that Bill could see who had fiddled with the records.

She spotted Pam Greeley down at the other end of the hall, getting her books out of her locker. Cathy headed in that direction through the crush of students, trying to make her approach look casual. "Hi, there," she said, as soon as she came within earshot.

Pam jumped and snapped her head around. Cathy noticed that the pupils of Pam's eyes appeared larger than the dim lighting of the corridor could account for. *Is she speeding right now? Has she been doing it all along, and I've never noticed?*

Cathy gave the cheerleader what she hoped was an ingratiating smile, and she pulled at the red and blue scarf around her neck. "Hi," she said again. "It's only me."

"Hi," Pam replied. "What brings you over here, Booster Girl?"

"Just checking in, that's all," Cathy said. "You told me yesterday that you were going to introduce me to the Booster Buddy."

Pam looked uncertain. "Ah . . . I don't know. Why are you in such a hurry to meet him?"

That was a question Cathy hadn't expected. "I was planning to take the afternoon off, and I wanted to make sure I was covered," she replied, thinking fast. "I have a couple of things I have to do."

"Oh, if that's all," Pam said, adjusting the knot in her own Booster scarf, "don't worry about it. That's all taken care of automatically. And the Buddy will introduce himself to you when he's ready."

"It would be really good if it was this morning," Cathy persisted. "If I had some of those Booster Bucks, I could go shopping."

"We can't talk here," Pam said. The first bell for homeroom rang as she spoke, and she hurried off. Cathy watched her go, then shrugged. She'd have to cut class without meeting the Buddy and hope that the Boosters' absence-protection program gave Bill enough information to do his part of the job.

After lunch, she decided, as she headed to her own homeroom. *Mom's going to be out then, so I can head straight home without having to invent some kind of phony reason for showing up early.*

The rest of the morning went by at a pace she'd previously thought reserved for the advance of glaciers and the decay of radioactive waste. Cathy fretted silently, wishing that this whole mess would hurry up and be over. None of the things the Boosters had offered her—faked report cards, days away from school, even money—were worth acting like a friend to these people. Cathy was sure now that they had killed Jennie, and seeing justice done for Jennie's sake was more important than any amount of Booster Bucks.

She wouldn't have to play along much longer, thank goodness. Once Bill got the Boss's name and passed it along, she'd cheerfully call up Detective Rogers and let him do the rest. Just the same, lunch that day was hard to take. Looking at the cheerleaders with their scarlet and blue Booster scarves, and the sweating jocks with their bright, dilated eyes, Cathy had to force herself to eat. She was happy that her thick glasses hid the expression on her face.

At the end of the meal, she caught Pam's eye and said, "I'm taking off now," and left. She made her way out of the school and down through the student parking lot. It wouldn't do to have Mr. Lipton or

Mr. Cooder look out the front windows of Cresswell High and see her standing at the bus stop out front.

Instead, she walked a few blocks out of her way and caught the A bus toward downtown Cresswell, then took a transfer and made her way back to her family's house in the Upper Basin. When she got there she saw that the pickup was missing from the curb out front. That was good, she thought; it meant her mother wasn't home. Cathy could go in unnoticed and wait by the phone for Bill to make his call. By evening, the nightmare would be over.

Cathy unlocked the door and went in. She hung up her coat on the rack in the front hall, dropped her books onto the hall table, and walked into the kitchen, flipping on the light. Then she halted, one hand still on the light switch. She didn't know what had alerted her—a sound, a smell, some half-noticed object moved from its usual place—but she knew that something was wrong. The house didn't have the feeling that an empty house has. She wasn't alone.

"Mom?" she called.

But it wasn't her mother who came in from the living room. "Hello, Booster Girl," Matt said.

Cathy looked about wildly, only to see Eric Skidwell coming down the stairs behind her. The two boys came nearer, smiling, pressing close.

Eric held up a slim piece of metal. "After someone got into Bill's car trunk, and Jennie's house, and your locker, and Don's house, maybe you should have figured out that someone knew how to use a lockpick."

Then Matt reached up and gently took Cathy's glasses off her nose. The room unfocused, leaving her isolated amid a blur of indistinct colors, in which she could make out shape and movement but little more. She heard her glasses drop to the wooden floor, then saw a fuzzy motion and heard the lenses crunching under a descending foot.

"We're real sorry about this," Eric said behind her, "but the Booster Club thinks that you're planning to tell their secrets."

"No, no! I promise—" Cathy felt numb, as if this weren't really happening to her, as if it were happening to someone else, like Jennie, or Don.

Eric laughed. "Too late for that," he said. "You know what happens to people who tell the Booster Secrets. You swore 'hope to die,' remember?"

Cathy heard noises outside the kitchen—the front door opening and closing. "Mom!" she cried out. "Help!"

More laughter answered her, and Todd Barber's voice, saying, "Am I too late?"

"Don't worry," Matt replied. "The party's just starting. And we're *all* going to have some fun!"

They're speeding. They must be. There's no way to talk to them, reason with them.

She made a dash for the kitchen wall phone. She could find that in the dark if she had to. Just dial 911 and yell for help, and the police would be here in no time flat. She grabbed the handset and pressed the receiver to her ear.

Nothing. No dial tone. No sound except the Boosters laughing.

"Oh, Cathy, you should see the look on your face," Eric said. "It's priceless. We cut the phone line, you dumb cow!"

In that moment, a cold fury replaced Cathy's panic. A memory came to her of what her father had said: *"You both know where I keep the shotgun—and before I leave on this run, it'll be loaded."*

The hall closet . . .

She couldn't let them know what she was trying, though, or they'd stop her. *I have to fake them out somehow,* she thought, and made a dash toward the back door. She almost got there, but two of the colored blurs moved at the last minute to block the way.

"Haven't you ever seen us play?" Eric's voice asked. "We're *good* at blocking."

Cathy turned away, stumbling as she did so, and collided with a corner of the kitchen table. She heard Matt laugh as she ran again, as if heading for the front door. Another moment, and the closet door was beside her. She pulled it open.

"Wrong door, Atmore," Todd snorted. "That isn't the way out."

Please, God, let the gun still be in here, Cathy prayed as she heard the Boosters laughing behind her. Then she felt it under her hands, a long shape of cold

133

metal and polished wood. She grabbed the double-barreled W. W. Greener twelve-gauge from the closet, turned toward the Boosters, and pulled back both hammers with her thumb. There was a loud click as the weapon cocked.

Nobody was laughing anymore. There was silence, broken only by quick, excited breathing from the Boosters and by Cathy's own pulse thundering in her ears. The Booster boys were a mass of colored shapes, keeping a respectful distance from the shotgun. With her back still pressed against the wall, Cathy slid sideways until she stood in a corner of the living room, where anyone coming at her would have to come from the front.

She pointed the muzzle of the shotgun at the center of the blurred mass that represented her classmates. "I don't have to see you to shoot you with this," she told them, swinging the side-by-side barrels to track the nearest moving blur. "All I have to know is where to point."

From somewhere in the room, she heard Eric's voice. "You won't get away from us, Atmore."

She swung the muzzle toward the sound. "I've seen you block," she said, and to her surprise her voice didn't crack. "Now, I want to see you *run*."

Everyone froze for a long moment. Then the colored blurs began moving again, drifting slowly out of the room and into the front hall. Cathy heard the front door open, then the sound of footsteps, heavy and light ones, going away. Out in the street, a minute or so later, a car roared off with a screech of peeling rubber.

Cathy stood and waited, the buttstock of the twelve-bore clasped against her hip. At last the only sounds were her own breathing, and the only motion the rippling of light from the outside windows. The house felt truly empty now, for the first time since she'd come home.

She left her place in the corner. Still holding the shotgun with her finger on the pair of triggers and with one shoulder touching the wall to guide her, she went to the front door, locked it, and put on the chain. She went into the kitchen and bolted the back door, and then groped her way upstairs.

In her room, she felt around in the bottom drawer of her desk for the old pair of glasses that she kept there, and she put them on. With the world in focus again, she sat down on the bed, trembling. *Never mind Bill's proof. As soon as Mom gets back I'll go next door, borrow a phone, and call the police. If I tell Rogers that people cut my phone lines, broke into my house, and threatened to kill me, he'll have to listen.*

Just then someone started pounding on the front door.

Cathy jumped, then went downstairs, still clutching the shotgun, and looked out through the peephole in the door. Bill Madsen stood outside on the steps.

"What do you want?" she called through the door.

"There's something I saw on the net, when I was looking for the Booster Boss," Bill said. "I tried to call, but your phone was out. I wanted to warn you. The Boosters are coming after you. I got over here as quick as I could."

Cathy let out a sigh of relief. "Boy, am I glad to see you," she said. "But you're a little late. They were just here, but I scared them off."

"Then let's go talk to the cops," Bill said. "My car's right across the street."

"Okay, good idea," Cathy said. "I'll be so glad when this whole thing is over."

She took the chain off the door, opened it, then stepped outside. After turning her key in the lock, she went across the street with Bill, still holding the shotgun and never minding what the neighbors thought. When they reached the car, Bill unlocked the passenger side and Cathy got in, sliding the shotgun onto the floor beneath her feet.

Bill got behind the wheel of the Ford and pulled away from the curb. After a bit Cathy looked around.

"Hey, wait a minute," she said. "This isn't the way to town."

"No, it isn't," Bill agreed, and kept on driving.

"But you said—"

Cathy never finished the sentence. Instead, she stopped short at the sound of a laugh from the back seat. Strong hands pinned her shoulders to the seat. Jerking her head around, Cathy saw Eric and Todd pushing aside the folds of the olive-drab army blanket that had hidden them.

"Surprise, Booster Girl," said Eric. "We're all going to Johnson's Swamp. But not all of us are coming back."

Chapter 14

Cathy twisted in her seat, trying to work free of the hands that held her so she could reach the door. Better to break some bones throwing herself out of a moving car than to die with her throat cut in Johnson's Swamp. But Eric and Todd had too strong a grip on her shoulders and upper arms, and all she could do was squirm.

"Don't flail around so much, okay?" said Bill. "You might make me have an accident before we get there."

Eric snickered. His breath was hot on the back of Cathy's neck. "We don't want that, now, do we?"

Bill drove on, down through the Lower Basin and out past the industrial buildings on the edge of town. He turned off the highway onto a narrow dirt road—the same one, Cathy felt certain, that those two hunters had taken not many days before—and pulled into a grassy turnout where Matt's BMW was already parked. Cathy recognized the exact spot where the television reporter had stood as he told the citizens of Cresswell that a teenage girl had been found murdered in the depths of Johnson's Swamp.

Tomorrow or the next day, he's going to be back out here again. Cathy could imagine the trench-coated and blow-dried announcer standing with his microphone at the very same spot, talking in his rich baritone about the unfortunate fate of yet another Cresswell High teenager.

"I should never have trusted you," she said to Bill. "The police were right all along."

"Call it a learning experience," said Bill. "Sometimes appearances aren't deceiving."

" 'Learning experience,' " laughed Todd. "That's great. You learn something every time . . . you know what I learned, with Jennie?"

"Haven't the foggiest," said Bill as the Ford rolled to a stop next to the BMW. "Enlighten me."

"It's really neat," said Todd. "When your throat's cut, and you try to scream, nothing comes out— nothing but blood, that is."

"Good point," said Bill. He turned to Cathy. "If you're going to scream, you'd better do it now."

She tried to spit at him, but her mouth was too dry. "Get stuffed, Madsen," she said bitterly.

"Okay," said Bill, "that does it."

He opened his door and stepped out. Then he pulled the shotgun from under Cathy's feet. A few feet away, the doors of the BMW opened, and Matt came out, followed by Pam and Stacy. The little group converged on Bill, as he stood with the shotgun cradled loosely in his arms.

Bill looked from one Booster to the next. "I called you here because we have another traitor," he said.

"She wouldn't get the signals, so it's time to send another message."

"Wait a minute," Matt said. "You told us back at the Atmores' that you were the Booster Boss. But we still haven't seen any proof."

"You're here because I told the Booster Buddy to call you here," Bill replied. "Isn't that proof enough for you?"

Matt wasn't satisfied. "If that's so, then why did you have us hide Jennie's legs in your mom's car?"

"So the cops would find out and arrest me," Bill said. "If I go to trial and get acquitted, they can never try me again on the same charge, no matter what new evidence they come up with later. Not even if one of you talks. But you *won't* talk, will you? We all know what happens to Boosters who blab."

He nodded toward Todd and Eric. "Bring Atmore over here."

Stacy looked at Pam. "I told you she didn't have what it takes to be a Booster," she said. "She's another goody-goody, just like Jennie turned out to be."

"Yeah," said Eric. "And 'just like Jennie' is the way it's going to go from here on out. Todd, you did the knifework on Jennie, so you have to take care of Cathy, too. That way the cops will see that it was done by the same person and keep on looking for just one guy. We don't want them to start getting ideas about some kind of conspiracy."

Matt grinned at Todd. "Looks like you get lucky again."

"Yeah," Todd said. He pulled a switchblade from his pocket and flicked it open. "Matt, you want to get your hacksaw while I get started?"

"Hold it, Matt," said Bill. He swung the shotgun to point at Matt and Eric. "I want you to let her go. Now."

There was a moment of frozen silence. Then the two football players dropped their hands from Cathy's shoulders, and she pulled away. Bill swung the gun a fraction to cover Todd. "Drop the knife, Booster Boy. Cathy, get over here. You, Matt, take out your car keys!"

"What is this? What's going on?" Pam said.

Matt started digging in his pocket for his keys, but Todd didn't drop the switchblade. He was still looking at Bill with an incredulous expression on his handsome features. "You mean you really *aren't* the Booster Boss?"

"Two points for Mister Genius!" Bill said. "No, I'm not the Booster Boss. I'm the guy who broke your code and told you to come down here so I could see who you were." He pointed the shotgun back at Matt. "Now toss your keys into the swamp."

"Don't do it, Matt," Stacy said.

"Shut up," Bill said.

Looking choked with anger, Matt flung the keys away from him. The small bits of bright metal flew through the air in a glittering arc and splashed down into a puddle of muddy water. In that same instant, Todd Barber bent over and stabbed the switchblade into the sidewall of one of the tires on Bill's old

Ford. Air hissed out, and the corner of the car began to sink.

"Okay, smart boy," Todd said, tossing the knife from hand to hand. "Now you're stuck here with us. You don't have the guts to use that gun—if it's even loaded." He took a step closer to Bill, then suddenly lunged forward, knife extended.

A booming sound echoed across the water of Johnson's Swamp. Then there was Bill, looking kind of surprised, and Todd, lying on his belly in the grass. The pellets from the shotgun had hit him full in the face, and blood, brains, and hair were spattered now in a wide arc behind where he had stood. Pam stood silently, wide-eyed and pale with shock. Stacy pointed uncomprehendingly at Todd's body, then began to giggle, softly at first, then more uncontrollably.

Cathy was the first to unfreeze. She grabbed Bill's arm and pulled. "Come on, let's go!" she shouted into his ear.

All at once everyone was either running or yelling. Cathy headed off into the underbrush surrounding the swamp, Bill at her heels, while Pam and Stacy finally began to scream. The last thing Cathy saw before the shrubbery blocked her view was Matt on his hands and knees, groping in the water where he had tossed his car keys.

After that, Cathy and Bill ran blindly, not looking back. The swamp was full of dense underbrush, broken up by stretches of shallow water and hummocks of marsh grass. The thick, foul-smelling mud clung to their feet, as if trying to slow them and drag them down. Wild birds burst skyward out of the bushes as they floundered past, and every rustle and whir of wings sounded to Cathy like the noise of pursuit.

Finally, she and Bill paused to catch their breath. Cathy had no idea how far they had come since breaking away, but she knew they'd been running for a long time. They looked it, too, with water dripping from every fold of their clothing and their shoes squishing when they walked. Cathy's hair was tangled with weeds and twigs, and mud caked her arms up to the elbows from when she had tripped and fallen face-first into a pool.

The sun hovered on the western horizon, and a cold wind had blown up out of the northwest. Now that Cathy was no longer running, she began to shiver—partly from cold, and partly from the aftermath of what she had just witnessed.

"Now what?" she asked, her teeth chattering. "I think we've lost them for a while."

"We're not out of trouble yet," Bill said. "This gun is double barreled. The Boosters have to know we've got only one round left, and they know that if we get away, they're all going to jail forever."

"So what are we going to do?"

"Beats me," Bill replied wearily. He leaned back against a broken tree stump. "Your turn to have ideas. I'm fresh out."

Cathy stared at him. "You mean you pulled this whole thing without knowing what you were going to do next?" she demanded.

"I didn't have time to think of anything better," Bill said. "I was playing everything by ear and trying to get one of the Boosters to confess, just like what happened. The rest was, well, an accident."

"You didn't think about calling the cops yourself?"

"Of course I did," said Bill. "But Detective Rogers was out of the station, and I had to leave a message with one of his flunkies. Is it my fault it didn't get through? There really was a message telling the Boosters to kill you—I was too late to stop it going out. So I had to add some stuff setting up that meeting in the swamp, then pass the word to Rogers and hope the cops would be here when the Boosters showed up."

"Well, they weren't."

Bill gave a tired shrug. "So sue me. I can't roll aces all the time. By the time I got to your house, the Three Stooges were already running out the front door. I had to talk real fast to convince them that I was one of the Boosters and not a possible witness for the prosecution. Things were happening too fast for me to cover all the angles."

"Oh, well," sighed Cathy. "Why *did* Eric and Todd put Jennie's legs in your car?"

"I think the Booster Buddy was trying to frame me, because he figured I knew enough about the computer net to find him and stop him."

"Oh. Then did you find out who the real Booster Boss is?"

Bill hesitated for a moment. "No. But I managed

to break his code. That's how I told everybody to show up at the swamp, and that's how I convinced Todd and Eric that I was the guy. I really thought I was going to be able to lead the cops right to them."

"All right," Cathy said, getting to her feet. "If it's up to me to have ideas now, I say let's head for the lumber mill. It's down around here somewhere, and maybe there's someone there who can help us."

Night had fallen by the time Cathy and Bill got down to where they thought the lumber mill was. Cathy couldn't feel her feet anymore from the cold water, and Bill was staggering. They came out onto the road, but the lumber mill was nowhere in sight.

Bill shook his head. "I knew there was a reason why I should have joined the Boy Scouts."

"Don't worry about it," Cathy said. "Now that we're on the road, we can find the town."

"Or the Boosters can find us."

"If we see them, we'll hide," Cathy said with more confidence than she actually felt. "Look, they won't do anything where there are witnesses. All we have to do is find some real people, and we're safe." She pointed northeast, where the skyglow of downtown Cresswell illuminated the bottoms of the low-hanging clouds. "Town's that way. Let's start hiking."

They walked down the road in silence for several minutes. This far out of the city, no streetlights broke the darkness, but they could see the road as a pale strip between the deeper shadows of woods on either side.

"So tell me what else you know," said Cathy at last. "I haven't got much myself. I never did learn who the Booster Buddy is."

"It's okay," Bill said. "I figured that part out this morning. It has to be Stu Martin. When he goes into the computer net, he has a particular style, and I recognized it."

Cathy thought back to Stu's argument with Larry, to Stu's mysterious conversations with Pam Greeley and Mark Metzger, to Stu's surprise at seeing her in school the day Don died. *No wonder he was surprised. I was supposed to be lying dead out in Gaspee Farms.*

"I should have figured that out from the start," she said aloud. "He was in all the wrong places with all the right people."

"But he's only the Boosters' pet hacker," said Bill. "He was taking his orders from someone else who talks to him through the computer network."

"Watch out," Cathy cut in. "There's a car coming."

The headlights of the approaching vehicle illuminated the telephone wires overhead, making them into strings of silver against the dark. Cathy looked around. Nowhere to hide. "Get ready," she said.

"I am ready," Bill replied. "With any luck it's an honest citizen going about his lawful business. He'll see two filthy teenagers walking down the road carrying a shotgun, put his foot down hard on the accelerator, and call the police from the nearest pay phone."

"I'll take it," said Cathy. "As long as I'm inside a

nice bright room with central heating, I'll explain that shotgun to the cops until they're sick of hearing about it."

But the car was slowing. It came to a halt on the shoulder up ahead and began backing toward them. Cathy held her breath. Next to her, Bill had his finger on the trigger of the shotgun.

The car stopped, and the driver reached over to open the passenger-side door. The domelight on the inside came on, lighting up his face. What Cathy saw wasn't exactly the honest citizen she'd been hoping for, but he wasn't a Booster, either.

"Henry O'Toole!" she exclaimed. "I never thought I'd be glad to see you!"

"That's my life in a nutshell," Henry said. "Can I give you a lift anywhere?"

"Oh, please," said Cathy. "Could you take us to the police station?"

"*To* the police station?" Henry shook his head. "There's no accounting for some folks' taste. But if that's what you need—jump right in."

Cathy and Bill got into the car, Cathy in the front and Bill in back. As soon as they were settled, Henry put the car into gear and started down the road to Cresswell.

"So what are you two guys and a major-league firearm doing all the way out here?" Henry asked at last. "Car break down on the way to a shotgun wedding?"

"Actually, we're trying to avoid some people," Cathy said.

"You sure picked a good place to do it," Henry said. "Are the people you're trying to avoid Eric and Matt and all those guys?"

"How did you know that?" Bill asked nervously.

"Because they're cruising all over the place like they're looking for someone," Henry replied. "For that matter"—he looked up in his rearview mirror—"I think I see Matt's car behind us now."

"Oh, no," Cathy said. "Bill, better duck down."

She slid herself lower in the seat so that her head didn't show above the windows. The headlights behind them swept up, then around and past.

"Better stay down like that," Henry advised. "Those guys are all over the place. That's, like, the third time I've seen Matt tonight." A few minutes later, Henry announced, "Coming into town. Stand by for lots of streetlights. By the way, what did one street say to the other?"

"I don't know," Cathy said.

" 'I'll meet you at the corner.' Gee, just what I always wanted—a captive audience.

"Anyway, these two cannibals are having dinner, and one of them says, 'Your wife makes really good soup,' and the other one says, 'Yeah, but I'm going to miss her.' "

Cathy groaned inwardly. *I'm really paying for this ride. But it's better than being stabbed to death.*

They drove on. Streetlights flickered by on either side as they drove. In spite of Henry's jokes, Cathy found herself growing more and more tense. She couldn't tell where they were—she had no clear idea of the route by which they'd entered town—and she didn't dare stick her head up to look for a landmark. All she could see through the top of the windshield was the night sky, empty except for the flashing red light of the *Eyewitness News* traffic helicopter.

"It won't be long now," Cathy muttered to herself. "A few more minutes, and it'll all be over."

"That's right," Henry said. Then he began to hum under his breath—no words, just a tune. But Cathy knew the words he'd put to it that day in the cafeteria, before Don Fulman had shut him up.

Jennie Brodie's bloody body's bundled in a body bag,
Jennie Brodie's bloody body's bundled in a body bag.

The car made a right turn, slowed and stopped. Henry stopped humming.

"We're here," he announced.

Abruptly the car doors were jerked open from the outside. Rough hands reached in and pulled Cathy and Bill out onto the pavement. In the light of the headlights from a circle of cars, Cathy saw that she and Bill were in the open courtyard of the Boosters' secret meeting place, surrounded by Boosters Matt and Eric and Pam and Stacy and all the rest. Stu Martin was there too—and Henry O'Toole, leaning back and grinning and holding the shotgun.

" 'Gory, gory Jennie Brodie,' " he murmured, and shook his head. "Some folks just *never* learn."

Chapter 15

"*You're* the Booster Boss?" Cathy asked. She supposed she ought to be frightened, but the past few hours had left her too drained for any emotion but a sort of weary disbelief.

" 'Tell me not, sweet, I am unkind,' " Henry said, bowing low and sweeping off an imaginary hat. "My pal Stu, here, will vouch for me."

"So Martin *was* your tame hacker," said Bill. His face was pale in the glow from the ring of headlights. Deep shadows in his eye sockets and along his jawbone made him look almost skeletal, but his voice didn't sound much different from the way it usually did—calm, and just a little contemptuous. "You should have picked somebody who was better at covering his tracks. Or was Stu the only one dumb enough to play along with a no-win game?"

"Talk all you want," said Henry. "The only losers are going to be you and Cathy. The way I see it, you were busy taking Cathy apart when Toddie-boy caught you in the act. That's when you shot him in the head, naturally—but he still managed to nick you first."

"And I suppose I'm going to bleed to death before I can get medical attention," said Bill. "Not bad, but I hope you realize a good pathologist could find more holes in that story than in a lace curtain."

"That bothers me not at all," Henry said. "The cops will buy it because they can mark the whole case 'solved.' And even if they don't, so what? They won't be a step nearer to knowing who did what and with which and to whom."

"Let's get on with it," said Matt. His eyes glittered in the glare of the headlights. "I want to make them hurt for what they did to Todd."

"Before you turkeys do anything dumber than you already have," Bill said rapidly, "you might want to look in my right-hand jacket pocket."

"You're stalling," said Henry. "But what the heck —I'll give you points for a good try. Check it out, Pam."

The cheerleader looked nervous and trembly, her pupils wide and dark. She went over and felt inside Bill's jacket pocket, and she pulled out a small tape recorder. "What are you doing with this?" she asked.

"It's voice-activated," Bill said. "I use it to help take notes in class—I forgot, you wouldn't know anything about classes. You should try going to one someday. You might learn something. Now play the tape."

"There isn't a tape," Pam said.

"What a surprise," said Bill. "Of course there isn't a tape. That cassette has your confessions on it

151

from down in the swamp, and it's hidden where you'll never find it—but the police certainly will."

He was bluffing, Cathy knew; they hadn't paused in their headlong flight long enough to hide anything. But she couldn't help admiring his nerve, and even Henry O'Toole seemed to feel a bit of reluctant appreciation.

"Sorry," Henry said. "But I'm the only one who's allowed to tell jokes around here."

"It's no joke," Bill said calmly. He paused. "Unless you want to laugh your way right onto Death Row. Every single one of you is old enough to be tried as an adult—and the jury won't have any sympathy for a bunch of rich kids who got their jollies from drug-trafficking, extortion, and cold-blooded murder."

He turned to Stacy, looking at her until she met his eyes. "Maybe you should try to cut a deal, tell Detective Rogers everything you know, and hope he'll go easy on you. But if you're going to cut a deal you'd better do it quick, before the rest of your buddies decide to make you the next corpse."

"Enough talk," Henry cut in. "I'll take my chances with that tape, because personally I don't believe it even exists. Are you ready, Matt?"

Matt pulled out a knife. "Any time you give the word, Boss."

"Actions speak louder than words," said Henry. He smiled happily at Bill, Cathy, and the Boosters. "I want to hear some actions, and I want those actions to scream!"

Matt stepped up to Cathy, so close that she could feel his breath on her face. "You first," he said hoarsely. "A little bit at a time. Let's see how long you can keep on making noise."

Cathy closed her eyes. *I'm sorry, Jennie. I tried, I really tried.*

But she didn't feel the knife. An amplified voice shouted "Police raid! Hands up!"

A moment later a blaze of white light struck against her closed lids, and the air was full of the loud *whop-whop-whop* of helicopter blades.

She opened her eyes. Most of the Boosters had frozen in the sudden glare of light, their hands above their heads. Only Henry moved. He spun around, bringing up the shotgun, and fired it upward into the night. From out of the dark, a weapon barked and flashed in return. Henry crumpled to the brick pavement, the shotgun falling from his hands.

Police were suddenly all over the scene, handcuffing all the Boosters. Henry was lying on the ground next to Bill and Cathy. His breath came in harsh gasps. "Aren't I the lucky one," he said, coughing. "They're going to serve Breaded Veal Cutlet tomorrow at school, but *I* won't have to eat it."

Then his body was racked by spasms and he vomited blood, thick and dark like coffee grounds. He gasped again and lay still.

Detective Rogers walked up. "Okay, you two," he said to Bill and Cathy. "Want to tell me what you're doing here?"

"Gathering evidence," Bill said. He reached into

his left jacket pocket—not the right one, which Pam had searched—and pulled out a tape cassette. "Here's a recording of these guys confessing to killing Jennie Brodie. What are *you* doing here?"

"Arresting some drug-dealers and murderers," Rogers replied. "I got your message this afternoon and went over to the Atmores' house. When we got there, we found that the front door lock had been manipulated and the phone line cut. There were signs of a struggle inside, and the shotgun was missing. We went down to Johnson's Swamp and found your car and a body. Ever since then, we've been looking for you."

"How did you find us in time?" Cathy wanted to know.

"Got a tip from a kid named Larry Davidson," said the detective. "He said the person we needed to look for was this Henry O'Toole guy. Our helicopter unit spotted him down on the Mill Road, and after that it was just a matter of waiting for enough backup."

Cathy blinked. "Larry?"

"I talked with him last night before I talked with you," Bill said. "And this afternoon I used the computer net to send him a copy of everything I'd figured out, before I went to your place: He must have worked the rest of it out from there while we were up to our necks in swamp water."

"That's right," said Detective Rogers. "And as soon as he'd figured it out, he started calling everybody he could think of at the police department.

Wouldn't give up until somebody listened. Unlike some other whiz kids I could mention."

"I didn't have any more time to waste making phone calls," Bill said defensively. "I was afraid they'd kill Cathy before anybody could get there to help."

"Be that as it may," Detective Rogers said, "that stunt of yours was dangerous as hell. Amateur detectives and amateur heroes aren't good for my ulcer. I ought to arrest both of you for attempted suicide." He paused. "Still, I have to thank you. If you hadn't acted, we might never have found out who was running the drug ring at Cresswell, or who killed Brodie and Fulman."

"You mean you don't think we're guilty?" Cathy asked, amazed.

"No," Detective Rogers said. "We have only a couple of things to wrap up. You'll have to come with me down to the station to give your statements. After that, you'll get a ride home in the squad car. It's all over."

Cathy looked from Henry O'Toole, lying dead on the ground, to the handcuffed Boosters lined up against a police van, and she knew that the detective was right. Whatever nightmares might linger in the aftermath of her involvement with the Booster Club, one particular nightmare would never come again. Jennie Brodie would cry no more in Cathy's dreams. Jennie had her justice now, and she could sleep.

OTHER TITLES IN THE HORROR HIGH SERIES
AVAILABLE FROM BOXTREE

☐ 1–85283–822–1 *Hard Rock*   £2.99
☐ 1–85283–827–2 *Sudden Death*   £2.99

All these books are available at your local bookshop or newsagent, or can be ordered direct from the publisher. Just tick the titles you want and fill in the form below.

Prices and availability subject to change without notice.

___

Boxtree Cash Sales, P.O. Box 11, Falmouth, Cornwall TR10 9EN

Please send cheque or postal order for the value of the book, and add the following for postage and packing:

U.K. including B.F.P.O. £1.00 for one book, plus 50p for the second book, and 30p for each additional book ordered up to a £3.00 maximum.

OVERSEAS INCLUDING EIRE – £2.00 for the first book, plus £1.00 for the second book, and 50p for each additional book ordered.

OR Please debit this amount from my Access/Visa Card (delete as appropriate).

Card Number | | | | | | | | | | | | | | | | |

Amount £ ....

Expiry Date ....

Signed ....

Name ....

Address ....